SECRET ARMY

THE END OF THE LINE

A Star Original

'Listen to me, Alain, carefully. Everyone in this apartment is infected with the bubonic plague – the Black Death. It is so serious that no one may come out until it is over. If there is anyone left.' He was suddenly wracked with a bout of coughing, and it was a moment before he could continue.

'If no one comes out in two days time you are to pour petrol under the door or throw the can into the room and set fire to it immediately. I mean that . . . You *must* let the whole floor burn thoroughly.'

'I can't just do that, Pascal . . .'

'You *have* to! There is no alternative . . .'

Also by John Brason

SECRET ARMY
SECRET ARMY DOSSIER

SECRET ARMY

THE END OF THE LINE

Based on the BBC-tv series

John Brason

A STAR BOOK

published by
the Paperback Division of
W. H. ALLEN & Co. Ltd

A Star Book
Published in 1979
by the Paperback Division of
W. H. Allen & Co. Ltd
A Howard and Wyndham Company
44 Hill Street, London W1X 8LB
Reprinted 1979

The cover photograph shows Clifford Rose as Kessler
in the BBC-tv production of Secret Army produced
by Gerald Glaister
BBC Copyright Photograph by Crispian Woodgate

Printed in Great Britain by
Hunt Barnard Printing Ltd., Aylesbury, Bucks.

ISBN 0 352 30535 5

For Bill Randle

Preface

Throughout the series SECRET ARMY we have based almost all the stories and characters upon actual persons and events. That applies to the stories in this book. Liberties have been taken, of course, in order to contain the story-lines within the framework of the series format, based, as it is, in Brussels.

For those who are interested in such things, the happenings of *Ring of Roses* occurred, not in Belgium, but in Northern France during October 1944.

The attacks on V-2 bomb-sites in *Just Light The Blue Touchpaper*, led by the fictitious Major Bradley, were actually masterminded by the late Airey Neave, M.P. and his colleagues. *The Execution* within the confines of an allied prison camp occurred, not outside Brussels, but in Schellingwoude, North of Amsterdam, in May 1945, five days after the end of the war in Europe. The actual Senior German Officer was later charged with murder by the relatives of the executed man.

Since the series has been shown in Belgium and the Low Countries we have received countless letters from viewers complimenting the production team on the startling authenticity achieved. It is our sincere hope that no one has been unduly distressed in reliving the happenings of the past.

The series was devised by Gerard Glaister and Wilfred Greatorex.
The Script Editor was John Brason.

JB 1979

JULY 1944

The Allied bridgehead in Normandy was not bogged down, but it did not rush across the French countryside like a mower across an English lawn either. The French held their breath. They understood, and did what they could. Four hundred miles away, in Belgium, it didn't look quite the same. They wondered what was happening – why it wasn't the all-conquering, all-consuming advance it just had *to be. They didn't understand. They were too inured against hope, too far into the German maw to permit of anything other than instant release. The Resistance continued their own private war. The evasion-lines quietly got on with scooping up Allied aircrew who dropped out of the skies, silently drawing them into their organisations and speeding them down their routes to Spain, to Switzerland, to safety. At least, they did until the Allied advance cut their routes through France and made a southern exit untenable.*

'Lifeline' was no exception. They could get their 'children' to Paris and the safe-houses in northern France, but beyond that was anybody's guess. It was pointless. They still kept coming. With Allied raids on Germany being stepped up all the time the number of shot-down aircrew was increasing, and, with nowhere to send them, the safe-houses were soon bursting at the seams. And – if truth were told – Allied High Command didn't really need them back. There was no longer any shortage of trained aircrew, or planes, or bombs.

'Lifeline' decided that the situation was impossible to maintain.

But as there was obviously no let-up in air-raids and therefore the numbers of evaders was continuing to increase, the men had to be put somewhere. It was Natalie who suggested that, at least while the weather was clement, the men could bivouac in the forests of the Ardennes. They could make themselves earths or wattle huts which would camouflage easily, and live rough for however many weeks it took before the victorious Allies swept into Belgium and liberated them from their spinneys. So it was. Within weeks more than three-hundred Allied aircrew were ensconced in forest earths, abandoned sheep-shelters, deserted barges in the Biesbosch flats, anywhere empty enough of people (especially Germans) where men could hide and exist without detection, either living off the land or receiving 'drops' of supplies when it could be managed.

But still they came. More flyers – British, Aussie, Polish, Indian, American, Canadian . . . from everywhere. All the evasion-lines were working to capacity . . . none more so than 'Lifeline'.

I

It was towards the end of July that Alain received a message to meet his old market colleague, Marc Savarin, in the Petit Poucet – an old café frequented by many of the market people. Savarin worked with Lifeline on a 'free-lance' basis. He could not be relied upon to be at the line's beck-and-call, which ruled him out as a regular. Not because he was unwilling or cussed, he was simply a man whose legitimate business took him about Ghent and Brabant and he was at no specified time in one place. But he had helped on more than one occasion and was trusted by them all. Yvette, the founder of Lifeline, had managed to pull him out of prison before the Gestapo got to him, and he had not forgotten his debt. When she was killed Marc Savarin renewed his membership in her memory, and Albert had been grateful for that reaffirmation.

He walked into the smoke-filled café and looked about him, spotted Alain chatting and laughing with some mates sprawled over a lurid pin-table in one corner, and sat down at an empty table. Soon Alain joined him. They shook hands, ordered kriek, and lit cigarettes as they waited for their neighbours in earshot to vacate their table. The moment it happened Savarin leant forward and fixed Alain with his brown eyes.

'Get a message to Albert, today. Tell him Paul Vercors knows about the Cherbourg massacre and is out to get him. There is a meeting tonight. I will find out all I can, but it is not easy. Make him understand they mean this. It is not an empty threat, Alain.'

They talked quietly for a few seconds longer before two old porters from the market sat down at the vacated table and stared in silence at the customers through tired and bleary eyes. They had been working since four. It was now almost noon.

Alain told Albert in the back room at the Candide during the late lunch period. As ever the restaurant was well patronised. Belgian well-to-do and blackmarketeers, and a dozen or more German officers, one of them a Generalleutnant. Albert was irritated at first by the intrusion.

'I can't talk now, Alain. For God's sake, man, the place is crowded.'

'It's your life I'm talking about, Albert. Suit yourself.' The tone of voice was enough to emphasise the words, and Albert turned to look at him as Monique put down the champagne-bucket and looked up.

It was Monique who spoke. 'What do you mean, Alain?'

He told them what Marc had said and added the snippets he had gleaned as they walked from the café.

'Look, Albert, Marc didn't have to tell us. He works with the communists as much as he works with us . . . '

'He isn't one and never has been. He's useful to us where he is, and he knows it. That's the only reason he sticks there.'

'I wouldn't count on political loyalties if I were you, Albert.' Monique warned. 'There's no love lost between Marc and the Hotel de Ville. He could be a nice warm pink.'

Alain shook his head. 'I trust him, anyway. He would do anything for Yvette . . . and Lifeline is still part of her as far as he's concerned.'

Albert considered for a moment. 'All right. I'll accept that he's doing what he can for us. What does it mean, then? A proper, full-dress assassination? Is that what they have in mind?'

'Marc will try and let us know. He promised. It's not easy for him, he's not part of the inner circle. Who's this bloke Vercors?'

'Paul Vercors was a member of Max's reseau. He was the one who sold-out the cello player to Kessler. He's a fanatic, and from what I've heard he intends to play a big part in the new

Communist Belgium he expects to take over when the Germans depart.'

'Fat chance! This isn't France. And it isn't going to be all that easy there, you mark my words . . . '

But Monique broke in, with the quiet insistence she showed now and again. 'Forget all that. Look, are we assuming that this is for real? Right, then we ought to prepare for it. The questions we need answers to are "How?" and "When?". Until we know that it's just a general warning to be on your guard.' She turned to Albert. 'And you better not go out alone. In fact why go out at all?'

'Because life goes on. Let's wait and see what Marc finds out. In the meantime we can start playing safe.'

Albert would carefully stash small arms conveniently about the Candide so that there was something useful within reach of the Lifeline people when they were on duty or about their business. A Luger in the wine-cupboard under the bar-counter – the little Smith-and-Wesson Natalie had given to her by Francois would tuck inside the piano, away from the strings, for Monique to grab if it should be necessary.

Alain offered to stay overnight at the Candide for a few days. Estelle was with her sister and had the children with her, but Albert thought it unnecessary and would draw attention to the fact that they knew something was on . . . which would spike the plan and possibly endanger Marc. No. They would continue in the normal routine and keep their eyes peeled. There was concern; not yet alarm.

They would have done well to consider the man Vercors. He was never obvious, he was never impulsive. He was cold, calculating, and he was vicious. He was also after revenge. Eighteen good comrades gunned down by the capitalist French police co-operating with their fascist oppressors was something he could not properly avenge . . . not yet. It was too impersonal and too far away. But the man who betrayed them was another matter entirely. He most certainly was a person, and he was in Brussels . . . and his name was Albert Foiret. That the massacred men had intended eliminating Albert Foiret and his immediate colleagues and taking over the resources of Lifeline as well as the organisation was neither here nor there. Crime is always legitimate in the cause of right, and right is always the way *you* happen to think. At least that is part of the communist creed, the bit that matters most, as history has shown and doubtless will do again.

But Vercors was nothing if not aware. He knew the chances of his pulling off a simple assassination, especially with the Germans in the city looking after their own – and to them, at least, Albert Foiret was one of them – was simply not on. What he needed to do, also, was keep London happy about the evasion-line so that their regular shipment of money would continue to arrive and fill the communist coffers. That necessitated the continuation of the line, and that, in turn demanded that the status quo was unruffled by anything very serious.

Now – if Vercors used his brains as he generally did – he could contrive to have Albert out of the way until such time as he could conveniently be got rid of, without panicking the London controllers into dropping everything. And it was this aspect that exercised his mind for several days before he hit upon the way of achieving his intent. It involved the police, and that was what appealed to Vercors. He liked that.

Marc managed to communicate to Lifeline that he had discovered that the assault on Albert was planned for July 29th and, as far as he could discover, during the evening. But that was all he could do.

When Albert shut up shop after the lunch trade on Friday July 29th, he busied himself checking the stronghold and saw to it that the concealed pistols were properly loaded (he had done this twice already). He slipped the safety-catches, then thought better of it, went round the house and peered out of windows, into the rear well-court. He even opened the sky-light from the disused attic and walked along the roof to check the side and rear walls for anything untoward. There was little noise above the Grand' Place, as if motorised vehicles had been banned from the city. There was little pedestrian traffic at that time of day. Albert reflected that before the war, in July, it didn't make any difference what time of day it was, the Grand' Place would be full of people either simply walking through or standing staring up at the magnificent square of buildings, their gilt ornamentation glinting in the summer light.

Albert paused and looked down the narrow building that was his. He had come a long way from a taxi driver who did not even own his own cab. The modest café in Ninove – also the 'Candide' – he had bought with his wife's money that he had inherited after her timely death the previous year. Almost immediately afterwards he got the chance, offered by London, to become part owner in the splendid restaurant in the Grand' Place where he now presided. One day, not so far away, all things being well, Albert Foiret would be *someone* in Brussels. A man to notice, to reckon with, to look up to. If he survived the war he would probably be decorated, known as a heroic patriot. Then, all things being equal, he might fulfil his promise to Monique and marry her.

He returned through the skylight and inspected the barred windows of the top two rear floors, and again the barred semi-basement ones at the rear which let onto the kitchens.

Vercors must be out of his mind if he thought he could assail the Candide. No, as long as they all kept their heads they would see it through.

Monique had made coffee for them in the back room. 'Surely they won't come during opening hours. I mean, the place is full of German officers, all sorts of people. They'd be recognised even if they got away. They won't try it, will they?'

Natalie was lying on the floor to rest her back which she had strained the week before when half-carrying a wounded evader from the farm truck to the bivouac area.

'I think they will. I remember what Max was like when he was determined to do something. Vercors will be the same. They all are. I *hate* communists almost as much as I hate the Germans.'

'Just be careful and don't let yourselves be flustered. We'll manage.'

'Can't we ask Paul Delon to send round a couple of men from the station? He'll help us if he can. I know he will.'

'I've asked him already.' Albert shrugged. 'He would were it not for the fact that all his men are out dragging a street with the SS. They found a small group of deserters in one house in the Rue Murillo, and then it was suspected that there were dozens of them hiding out . . . He can't help until the search is over.'

The hours passed nervously. Natalie managed to doze where she lay on the carpet. Monique attempted to do the week's accounts, and Albert did a totally unnecessary stock-taking while the kitchen staff were away from the place.

The cook, Pierre, arrived shortly after five and quietly got on with his chores. The others drifted in, one by one, totally unaware that there was anything afoot, conscious only that M'sieur Foiret was being fussy and hovering.

When the doors opened for the evening Albert was already tired and irritable, but the others suffered in silence. He was the target. He had a right to be edgy.

Customers arrived early these days. The first table was already eating at seven-thirty and a group of German officers arrived to take up their reservation at eight. It was going to be a good Friday night, off-putting for a would-be assassin.

By nine the place was three-quarters full, and Monique was preparing her make-up for her first stint at the piano. The pianist, Victor, had been playing background music since seven-thirty and was ready for a break.

Then they arrived. Separately, but at the same time. The first to come through the doors were three men of middle-age, possibly younger, who gave the impression of being irritable business men in the middle of a board-meeting. They were also very slightly drunk, or seemed so. The fourth person, separate from the others, was a sullen, burly man who seated himself near the door, then moved into the centre. The three business men had taken the long table exactly to one side of the entrance.

When Albert came from his office to the bar area Natalie

approached him and indicated the three new arrivals with her head.

'I don't like the look of those three. Why are they sitting near the door when there are still better tables?'

'Find out.' Albert was curt and his hooded eyes cold.

When she returned she shrugged unhappily. 'They seem to be just businessmen deep in argument about something. They won't move from the table, and they won't part with their brief-cases.'

'Are they bulky enough to hold guns?'

Natalie nodded. Albert considered, then he and Natalie went into the back room. He was nervous and prickly and undecided.

'I don't understand why we had to open at all. Wouldn't it have been more sensible to just get out of Brussels for a day or so?'

'You're not thinking, girl! How could we just close? The Germans would think it was suspicious immediately. The moment Monique or anyone isn't about Kessler or someone asks where they are. It's like being in the lime-light. We chose it that way, we have to stick it out. Besides, if they didn't make a hit tonight they'd try again. Let's just play it out.'

'What about the deliveries? There could be a bomb concealed . . . anything.'

Albert looked at Natalie. Normally she was the coolest of them all, despite the fact that she was always more upset than anyone if one of their number or friends was killed. Tonight she was on edge. He surmised it was being a sitting-duck, knowing it, and being unable to do anything about it. He felt the same way.

The evening wore on. Albert let his roving glance remain with the ones he didn't know, especially the group of three, and the one thickset, red-faced, open-pored man who tucked into his meal with the table manners of a hog. Albert felt that he knew him and, when the opportunity arose, introduced himself. The fat man turned out to be Inspector Benet of the Central Sureté –

a revelation that caused Albert to breathe out with more than a touch of relief. He pressed the policeman to extend his meal 'on the house' and plied him with wine and brandy for the rest of the evening, all of which the Inspector accepted without comment and tucked into. He had indulged in his habit of fastening the large napkin round his neck, which only further accentuated the bulbous, red and sweating neck above the linen.

An argument developed at the door table and the effect of too much alcohol began to permeate the Candide, causing customers to stare and mingle disapproval with anxiety. When the three left it was with the gentle urging of the proprietor and the tacit support of the red-faced policeman who glowered at them over his white crisp napkin and held up his card almost as if he were placing a bet or buying at an auction. It was enough. The men grumbled, picked up their cases and left. There was no fight, no threat, no planting for later. But within five minutes of their departure two leather-coated men with pulled-down trilby hats slid into the restaurant and surveyed the scene. The murmur of conversation dried instantly and the two Gestapo men continued their search of heads. Only twice before had these men ever entered the Candide. Like every city in Occupied Europe, Brussels had its fair share of these comic-opera characters. Their costume – the leather coat, almost to the ankles, and the slouch hat – lacked only a smoking bomb and a black mask to place them squarely into the chamber of ludicrous villainy, but no one in Europe smiled at them or their garb. They were for real, and millions of terrified people knew that to their cost.

Albert did not move. It was unlikely the communists would choose the rags of fascism for their agents, but one could not be certain. Stalin had got into bed with Hitler just prior to the war. Strange things happen when expediency calls the tune.

The two Gestapo men slowly walked across to a corner table and stood on either side of a Wehrmacht Oberst who had endeavoured not to turn when everyone else did. One whispered in his ear and the wretched man sighed, paled, and wiped his mouth on his napkin before standing up without speaking – the very picture of resignation. No one spoke. Albert did not move. In almost considerate silence the German officer walked stiffly from the restaurant escorted by the two angels of death. The purges were not over yet. The Hitler bomb-plot was still echoing throughout the garrisons of the Greater Reich. Albert swallowed and nodded to the pianist to break the silence and the tension. Monique joined him at the piano and sang a bright little French song that she had heard on the radio some weeks back.

The night wore on. The clocks ticked towards the curfew hour. Natalie continued to ply the now thoroughly roseate policeman with their second-best brandy, and one by one the customers departed.

Albert followed Monique into the back room, an unmistakeable sense of relief about his eyes.

'They're not coming. It was a false alarm . . .'

'Don't bank on that, Albert. The Ides of March may have come – they have not yet gone. I'm going to take a look round the kitchen and the back yard. You check the first floor and the men's toilet.'

Albert nodded, and accepted Monique's urging without comment. Natalie came in as Albert shook his rubber torch.

'That's everyone, except that fat policeman. Does he get a bill?'

'No, not this time. On the house. Tell him to come again.'

Albert checked every corner of the first floor, pulled the chain in the w.c., even moved the empty boxes in the corridor. There was nothing. He could hear Monique talking to the washing-up girls as she wandered about the basement.

'He wants to thank you, Albert.'

Natalie stood in the doorway and watched him coldly as he entered and replaced his torch in the drawer.

'Right, er, you go and give Monique a hand. I don't like her going into the yard alone.'

Natalie left and Albert straightened his tie before entering the now deserted restaurant and crossing to the table of the single remaining guest . . . Inspector Benet.

'I enjoyed myself, M'sieur Foiret. You run a first-class restaurant. Thank you.'

'Delighted to see you, Inspector. Please feel at liberty to come again, as my guest, of course.'

The policeman let Albert shepherd him to the doorway then turned to face him, smiling and offering his hand to shake. The moment Albert's right hand was extended the policeman, with surprising agility and great viciousness, pulled Albert's head forward and down as he brought up his knee. Albert's nose and that knee met with awful impact. The blood spurted across the door and floor and Albert almost sat back, stunned and helpless, but Benet twisted him with a sudden pull on the left shoulder of the jacket and sent him sprawling through the open doorway into the arms of two waiting gendarmes. The car drew away quickly and quietly.

When Monique returned to inform Albert that all was as it should be it was some minutes before she and Natalie realised that, despite everything, it had happened. From a totally unexpected source had come the villain. No shot had been fired, no fight engaged. She knew instinctively that Albert had been arrested, that it was serious, and that somehow it had been engineered by the communists and Paul Vercors.

It was the following day that Monique, using the services of Zander, Albert's notary, found that Albert had been arrested on a purely civil charge. The charge was murder.

2

Ring of Roses

July 26th fell on a Friday. Muissard wouldn't forget it all that easily . . . not for fifty years! Old Jean Jacques Muissard was unlikely to live another fifty years. He was seventy-three. Active, and even spry, but he was three over his allotted span and that fact was not lost on him. For three years he had turned out in the dark nights to probe about whenever there were suspected 'leaves falling'. He strained his ears above the darned and grubby pillow-slip for the tell-tale sounds of a descending aircraft. He got up whenever he heard anti-aircraft fire, however distant, and stood in his doorway and looked up into the black night and strained every nerve to see, smell, hear, or just sense that there might be an allied airman somewhere near Jean Jacques Muissard's old and dilapidated farm. But no, it was not to be. Not once had he found even a folded and half-buried chute, not, that is, until July 26th, at approximately eleven forty-six.

The old man had been out about a mile-and-a-half down the road watching, listening to no avail. He had stood in the warm evening air and watched the searchlights slowly extinguish their blue-pink fingers, heard the last muffled thunder of German flak before it, too, died, then turned silently away, chewing the broken stem of his ancient pipe, which he smoked upside down 'for blackout reasons'. It was when he got back to his farm gate that he noticed there was something odd about the old house. Somebody had stuck a damn great flag on his roof . . . no. It wasn't a flag. It was all white, and there was something fastened to the end of it.

Holy Mary! God in Heaven, and all the Saints! It was a parachute, and the weight on the end was man-shaped! Old Jean Jacques' prayers had been answered. He had his airman, and the Good Lord had dropped him right into the old man's lap.

The old farmer rushed up to the house and craned his neck to see better. It seemed as if the man was released from his harness all right, but one of the old iron brackets that stuck out and used to hold the old guttering before he had it moved had caught and torn the man's flying-jacket, and somehow had hooked him in such a way the poor devil was suspended, unable to get himself off the hook. Old Muissard blurted that he would fetch a ladder, and manage to get the man down efficiently enough and into his kitchen before any stinking Bosch would come sniffing around. He even managed to get rid of the parachute, but lost two chimney-pots in the process. Never mind! He had his airman.

When, next day, the old man handed the airman – an American who told him his name was McQuaig – over to his contact, he did so with tears of pride and achievement in his eyes, and embraced him several times before letting the farm-cart go on its way with 'his' aviator.

The safe-house McQuaig was taken to was in the Petit Place Astrid, an old street that ran off the Chaussee, long due for demolition and with only one house actually occupied. The absence of locals, and the out-of-the-way nature of the dilapidated street made it a splendid place to hide aircrew and also earned the safe-house the code name of 'The Ritz'. Shabby, and only just weathertight, it was nonetheless spacious (which most of the safe-houses were not) and permitted more internal movement than did the others.

There were five other aircrew already there. Two Yanks like himself, the rest Limeys. It seemed all so simple, so easy, so well organised, so confidence-making that McQuaig relaxed and would have felt on top of the world were it not for the stomach pains that assailed him now and again, the feeling of a fever coming on, and the wretched boil he was developing in his right groin. His compatriots were totally unsympathetic and ribbed him about it, but one of the Britishers who seemed to know his way about thought he was heading for gastric flu and persuaded him to stay covered in his bunk.

It was Tuesday morning when the nightmare started.

About four o'clock.

The telephone rang with its persistent, all-penetrating sound for several minutes before Monique grabbed her robe and heaved her weary body off the bed to flop down the stairs – and switch on the back-room light and grope in the sudden blinding illumination for the black hand-set.

'Yes? Candide . . . Who? . . . Yes, Marcel, how many? Not many of the hotels keep children any more, but I think the Ritz has a few vacancies . . . overnight or weekends. Yes, everything is fine . . . business as usual.'

She put down the receiver and sat down herself. It wasn't true. It was not 'business as usual' by any means. Albert had been taken by the police – the civil police, not the Gestapo – on some trumped up charge of having murdered his wife. It was nonsense of course. She was there when Andreé died. The poor woman had tried to get into her wheelchair, and work it to the head of the narrow stairway. Something had happened and all she and Albert knew was that they heard the clatter of something heavy falling down the stairs, a muffled scream, and then Andrée fell through the curtain and lay in a heap on the floor. She was dead. Her neck was broken. Now that communist bastard Vercors had perjured himself to the police and brought false witnesses to testify against her Albert. The upshot was the wretched man was incarcerated until such time as his attorney could extricate him from the clutches of the Examining Magistrate.

'Not another lot!' Natalie had been aroused by the telephone and the noise of someone talking. Monique sighed.

'I've put them in the Ritz at Koekelberg. We have to shift them out again immediately. You take four, I'll take the rest.'

But where to, Monique? All the safe-houses are full. There are over fifty in the Ardennes already. We'll need another two camps. What about the Biesbosch?'

'It's all very well. How do we feed them? They'll have to forage.'

Monique, suddenly reminded of the situation, decided to get another helper out of bed and get things on the move. She dialed Duval, the corn merchant, who helped them regularly by delivering food to their outlying safe-houses and, now, bivouacs. After a sharp exchange, mainly connected with the time of night, he agreed to get on with it on the morrow. That done, they returned to bed for another two hours.

Eugene Zander, notary, was also an early riser. Today he wanted to clear some of the backlog in his office before going to the Havenlaan Prison to visit his client, Albert Foiret. Even so, it was almost eleven before he entered the brick gateway and was shown to his client's floor, there to be escorted to the small interview room at the end of the cell corridor in 'A' Block.

Albert was already waiting for him, seated at a small wooden table. The warder remained by the door – outside – while the notary interviewed his client and introduced his companion, the dignified Advocate, Maitre Guissard, who he had retained for the case.

'This is Maitre Guissard, M'sieur Foiret. I have asked him to talk with you now so that he may consider the best course of action. The whole thing seems very odd to me.'

The advocate shook hands with his new client and seated himself opposite as Albert protested at the whole thing being a charade.

'M'sieur Foiret, the charge is quite serious, I assure you. The Prosecutor has more to do than play games. Certain charges have been laid by person or persons as yet unknown and undeclared to me. Bon. I have obtained from Zander your statement of the matter. I shall collect other statements and affidavits, if any. In due course the Prosecutor must reveal his hand to me and we will be able to assess the strength of the case. Bon. My, er, shall we say, preliminary sortie has indicated that the greater part of the case is circumstantial. It is not impossible to demolish this, but if we are to prove your innocence I will need all your assistance. Bon. You have, er, good relations with certain police officers?'

Albert glanced at Zander who merely shrugged the ball back into his court.

'Yes. One in particular. Inspector Paul Delon.'

'Then with your permission I will make good use of that relationship. Bon. So, shall we get down to work? First . . . answer me one question, M'sieur Foiret. Why did you *not* kill your wife?'

Albert stared at the man as if he were a lunatic.

'I am quite serious, m'sieur. You had plenty of reason . . . and opportunity. Please answer my question. It has bearing upon the defence.'

McQuaig started to feel ill about four hours after he arrived at the safe-house. It was a condemned house at the end of a row of dilapidated tenement buildings. The whole area was a honeycomb of narrow streets and demolition sites backing onto the old disused complex that had been Brussels's first, and main, gasworks. Now it was deserted and the whole area due for reclamation and development – after the war.

Their part of the house was a top-floor apartment consisting of two quite large rooms, an entrance hall and passage leading to a kitchen at one end, and a bathroom and lavatory at the other. There were eight evaders there now, five had been housed for roughly two days.

He had been persuaded to lie down on a dark palliasse and was now conscious of fever and the ensuing perspiration.

There was a coded knock at the landing door. Wade, an American navigator, rushed to the summons, replied with the code, and opened the door to admit Natalie with a basket of food.

'Thank God someone's come! We were beginning to think we'd been forgotten. Is everything all right?'

'We hadn't forgotten you, sergeant. But life is becoming rather difficult for us at the moment. We can't send you back to England because the Allied advance has cut our escape line. I can't imagine you want to try and get through the German front line *and* your own . . . '

'No way, lady. I'm for the easy life.'

'Well, it isn't going to *be* easy, I'm afraid. We have now sixty-three airmen living in camps in the Ardennes. There is no room for anyone to stay in safe-houses more than a couple of nights. There are just too many of you being shot down.'

'Wait a minute, you mean we have to live under canvas?'

'Well, maybe. In the forest, anyway. You will just have to wait until the Allied spearhead makes it possible for you to return to your units.'

Wade sidled up to her and slipped his arm round her waist. 'Can't I stay here with you, sweetheart?'

Natalie smiled and accepted the banter. She was used to it. It had grown steadily more overt as the war drew to a close and the Allied advance continued. There was conviction now in these flyers where once it had been only determination, and a rather unsmiling one at that.

'Someone else will be arriving shortly to guide you. She will take some, and I will come back for the rest.'

'She?' There was wide interest, real and forced. 'Is she pretty, too?'

'There is also a doctor coming to check you out if anyone needs it.'

She walked over to where McQuaig was lying. 'Are you feeling any better?'

'The same I think . . . I guess its just the boil thing in my groin . . . '

The reference to his swelling brought a roar of coarse comment from the others who had collected round him.

'If he's got a swelling where he daren't tell his mother we all know where he's been . . . '

'Dirty lousy lucky devil!'

Natalie jumped in to quell the noise. 'Quiet all of you. There is no one else in the house, but keep it quiet! This is Occupied Europe, a lot of people are putting their lives at risk for you!'

This last quietened them down quickly. The oldest and most serious of the group, Girton by name, spoke their feelings. 'I'm sorry, Miss. We really are grateful, you know. It's just a sort of safety-valve, you know?'

'I know, Lieutenant. I've been doing this for four years.'

The revelation brought forth a low whistle of incredulity.

'Four years! Can you beat that!'

The cell door was thrown back and Albert recalled to the interview room. On arrival he found Guissard waiting with Inspector Delon. Albert greeted his old friend with both hands.

'Paul! Thank you for coming.'

'I wanted Inspector Delon here to tell you himself what he has managed to unearth that I could not. Policemen have certain access . . . '

Guissard made a gesture that both implied a source, and invited Delon to unfold his findings.

'Maitre Guissard will have told you that the bulk of the evidence they have against you is circumstantial, supplied in the main by Madame Lekeu . . . '

Albert's face became grim. 'Celeste!' He spat the word with evident distaste. 'That bloody woman never liked me!'

'She is nevertheless on record with gossip and hearsay that she has embroidered into a serious statement. Even so, I knew she was not the sort to bring charges, nor was she the type to organise herself into doing anything. It had to be someone else. I took the liberty of asking your good friend Inspector Delon to look into it and find out *who* was responsible. I think you will find it interesting.'

Delon looked Albert straight in the eyes. 'It has to do with other activities . . . '

Albert immediately thumped the table with his fist. 'No.'

But Delon shook his head. 'Maitre Guissard already knows everything. It is necessary that he should in order to know what he should *not* unearth. You must see this, Albert. He is also a member of the Strombeek reseau.'

Albert eyed the advocate with renewed respect, but also with unease. 'He *knows*, Paul. That is one more danger!'

Guissard spoke quietly and reassuringly. 'You are correct, M'sieur Foiret. But there is no other way.'

Albert shrugged. He had resigned himself to the necessity.

Delon spoke to him again. 'Do you know the name Paul Vercors?'

Albert's eyes narrowed, he knew the name very well. He was the only surviving member of a communist reseau that Max Brocard, his one time pianist, had belonged to. One which had vowed to take over Lifeline for their own uses, and for which reason Albert had had Max and his comrades ambushed by the Germans and the French police. Vercors had survived by the simple expedient of not being there. He had been wounded slightly two days earlier when they blew up a railway track and the charge went off unexpectedly early. That accident saved his life, and it also meant that there was someone who wanted revenge upon Albert. So this was how! Albert already knew why.

The knock, when it came, broke up the conversation among the evaders and Natalie. She let in Monique and Doctor Keldermans then bolted the door behind them.

Natalie introduced them. 'This lady will be your main guide. As I told you you will be taken to a bivouac in the Ardennes area. This is our doctor. Does anyone need anything?'

'Only Mac over there. You saw him yourself, he doesn't look too good.'

Keldermans picked up his bag and followed Wade through to the other room and sat down on the bed by the recumbent McQuaig.

'Now lets have a look at you, my friend.' Quickly and with the expertise of forty-two years in practice Keldermans took his temperature and gave him a cursory examination. 'It's fever all right. How long have you had this?'

'Couple of days, doc. Sorry to gum up the works.'

But the old doctor was already peering interestedly at a patch of red skin appearing below the hairline and rising through it, and at another in front of his ear.

'Have you been fighting, or anything?' Then he answered himself. 'No, they aren't bruises.'

He turned to Wade hovering around behind his compatriot. 'Would you mind drawing back the curtain please. It isn't exactly bright in here . . . Mmh. Any other symptoms? Any nausea?'

'A little, sir. I just don't feel so good. I've been sick a couple of times, and, er, I'm passing a little blood, sir.'

'Stomach pains?'

'I guess so, not too bad, though. I think I'm getting a boil or something . . .'

He indicated the groin area with a movement of his hand, and Doctor Keldermans quickly undid his trousers to examine the swelling. After some moments the old man raised his head. It wore a distinctly puzzled look, and one eyebrow was raised. It was more than puzzlement. It was alarm mingled with disbelief. He turned round to face the others.

'Has anyone else any pains, sickness, lumps of any kind?'

Two of them glanced at each other, nodded, and informed Keldermans.

In the Security Headquarters on the Avenue Louise two officers were scrutinising a wall-map of Belgium and the Low Countries. Already the map was studded with pins. The officers were SS Sturmbannfuhrer Kessler, in charge of all SS, SD, and Gestapo activity in those areas, and Major Hans Dietrich Reinhardt, Luftwaffe Polizei, responsible for the capture of all Allied aircrew downed during raids on the Fatherland who parachuted or crash-landed in the same territory. Reinhardt was doing the pinning, Kessler reading from his report:

'. . . two in the area of Valkenburg, just east of Maastricht. Eight reported in Limbourg between Gruitrode and Elen. A total of seventeen aircraft. Five of them B.17s.'

'They will probably have come from the airfields in Italy or

North Africa. They do their bombing run and carry on to American bases in England.'

'Wasting fuel!' Kessler's scorn was evident.

'They have petrol to burn, Kessler.'

The SS Sturmbannfuhrer ignored the comment, knew it to be correct, but chose to appear indignant and pass it over. 'That is something like one hundred men in our area alone. What are they doing with them? We have not caught a single evader en route for weeks. Why?'

'We do not have enough men. Most of our vehicles are out of action due to lack of fuel. But there is something else we ought to consider.'

Kessler looked up at him and fixed his pale eyes on the Knight's Cross Reinhardt wore.

'Has it occurred to you that they might not be sending them back anymore? They can't send them south because of the fighting. If they try to get them out through the north it has to be by sea. Hundreds of men?' He shook his head. 'It is not practicable.'

'Men have been picked up off the Scheldt . . .'

'That was months ago.'

'It could well be that our security has made them give up their attempts.'

Reinhardt stared at his colleague in disbelief. Then exploded.

'Attempts? Their "attempts" have been eighty-six per cent successful! They have stopped sending them back because they don't need them, Sturmbannfuhrer! They have petrol to burn, trained flyers to abandon. They are knocking at our door, man. Why don't we go home?'

Reinhardt's voice had an edge to it that Kessler did not like. He could not, perhaps, fault Reinhardt's reasoning but his realistic acceptance of the obvious was more than the SS man could stomach. He decided to assert his authority.

'Major Reinhardt! You will take your full complement into the Limbourg area and scour the countryside for these *terror-fliegers*. Those are our orders.'

Reinhardt gritted his teeth and suppressed the answer he

would have liked to have given, but the SS was the SS, and he contented himself with sarcasm.

'Yes . . . sir. May I have some petrol for my vehicles, Kessler? Belgium is not a big country, but it takes eight men rather a long time to cover it on foot.'

Kessler turned on his heel and walked from the room. Reinhardt sighed and fastened his belt, then took his Walther pistol and a box of cartridges from the top drawer. He tipped out the contents of the box and started to chuckle, gradually letting his mirth grow into laughter. The box did not even contain one clip, just three solitary loose bullets.

Doctor Keldermans held down the tongue of the R.A.F. gunner with a spatula.

'When did you first feel the fever coming on?'

Shaw shrugged and buttoned up his battle-top.

'I didn't really think about it until you mentioned it, sir. I suppose we both felt the first sweats about dawn, when we woke up.'

'I see, thank you.'

He turned away, his face now drawn and grey, and about his eyes there was a distant look, almost a far-away concern that did not quite sort with the circumstances of the safe-house. Natalie had gone to attend to her end. Monique was busy about her charges, checking their false papers, giving them the best briefing she could in the time available.

'That's the last one, thank God.' She walked over to the doctor who seemed totally abstracted, even vague. She peered at him. 'Are you all right, Pascal?' He nodded and she continued. 'We could leave someone here with him if we have to, but it's another thing to worry about. I'd rather we moved him if we could.'

She turned away to move off but Pascal Keldermans touched her arm and his voice was urgent.

'Monique, do you have Albert's gun with you?'

'Yes. I shouldn't carry it, I know, but the searches have eased a bit. Why?'

The doctor held out his hand.

'Would you give it to me, please?'

She looked at him curiously, but took the weapon from her bag and handed it over.

'Is there a silencer?'

Again she looked at him queerly but delved into the bag and produced the cylinder. The old man took it without a word, screwed it into the pistol, checked the magazine, and, she noticed, slipped the safety-catch. Not at all sure what he was up to she watched him stand and cross to the door.

Without a word to anyone he shot the bolts, top and bottom, turned the key in the lock, and then bent down and pushed the key out under the door.

'Pascal! What on earth are you doing? We can't get out now!'

'I don't intend that any of us should.' The tall doctor looked across all the heads and raised his voice to speak with great clarity. His English was not all that good but he made up for his syntax in clarity of speech and emphasis.

'Listen to me – all of you. Does anyone know anything about McQuaig? Where did he come from, and when did he get here?'

It was Shaw who answered. 'We don't really know, sir. Other than he's a Yank, and he was shot down two days ago. He was too sick to talk much.'

'He did say it was his first mission.'

Keldermans sucked his goatee and made a face. 'I don't understand it. It doesn't make any sense at all.' He paused. 'I want you all to pay very close attention to what I have to say. This man McQuaig is not only very sick, he is almost certainly going to die.'

They were silent and shocked. Someone mumbled, 'poor chap,' but the response was silent in the main.

'I'm afraid there is more to it than that,' Keldermans continued. 'His sickness is highly infectious. We could all be affected. It is so serious that not one of us may leave this room.'

Protestations came quick and fast, varying from simple oathful comments to demands to come to his senses, or casting doubts upon the competence of continental medical practitioners. Monique broke through with her natural authority.

'Come on, Pascal, we've only just got here! We can't just leave them here indefinitely.'

'I don't think you fully understand, Monique. No one will be leaving anyone. No one, myself included, is leaving this room. I have locked the door and pushed the key outside. Unless we break down that door there is no means of exit.'

'Wait a minute! What's going on? I don't get it . . . ' Wade was not the only one who was confused, but Keldermans broke through with unaccustomed violence in his voice.

'Listen to me. Please! I am not talking about scarlet fever or whooping-cough. We have all been exposed to one of the most deadly bacteria known to man. How it can happen in this country, even in the squalor of wartime, I cannot understand. It is no longer endemic in Europe.'

The American stepped forward. 'I guess McQuaig need not have come from anywhere in Europe, sir . . . '

'Explain yourself.'

'Well, my hunch is that he was flying a B17 on the new milk-run. They only touch down in England *after* the mission.'

'Then, where would he have come from?'

'Italy, I reckon, North Africa . . . '

Keldermans face suddenly twisted into a grimace and his eyes closed for a moment. 'North Africa. Then my guess is more than a guess. It is a diagnosis and almost certainly correct. I wish to God it was not!'

Monique turned to look him in the face, apprehensive and irritated by the delay to her plans. 'What are you saying, Pascal?'

'What's he got, doc?'

Keldermans held the silence for a moment then very quietly made his dread announcement. 'Plague. Bubonic plague. There have been few outbreaks in Europe or civilised societies since the middle-ages. It used to be called the "Black Death". '

There was a chill intake of breath, and the faces looking at him had paled visibly.

'You have no doubt, Pascal?'

'None whatever.'

3

No one spoke except Wade who breathed out the word, 'Jesus!' Girton coughed nervously.

'But, how would he get it? Don't they have medicals?'

'It is transmitted by rat fleas. He would not know he had it, nor would anyone else until the symptoms started to appear, as they have done while he has been with us.'

'Well, Christ! Let's do something about it, get him to hospital.'

But Keldermans shook his head gravely.

'Quite apart from the question of safety and security – in the military sense – the danger of spreading is appalling. The risk is too great. With lowered resistance due to undernourishment, and an almost total lack of medical supplies it would spread like wildfire.'

Shaw, the burly gunner, made a movement towards the door. 'Well I'm not staying here . . .'

To everyone's shock and surprise Doctor Keldermans drew the gun from his pocket and without a flicker of hesitation fired at Shaw, putting a bullet into his leg. With a sharp yell of pain he fell to the floor, and Keldermans turned, gun-in-hand, to face the others.

'I'm sorry, I didn't want to have to do that. But I will empty this gun into whoever tries to leave, if I have to.'

Shaw lying on the floor turned his red and pain-distorted face to him and shouted, 'You can't kill us all!'

'No. But I am assuming that most of you are courageous enough to face reality and act with some sense of human responsibility.'

Wade shook his head as if to dispell the unreality of the situation. 'The doc's right. This is no clam bake. Keep talking, sir.'

Keldermans sighed. 'I'm trying to see all the permutations myself. Look, even if circumstances were normal, with everything functioning medically, the risk to the civil population is considerable. Several thousands could die before it was contained . . . children, babies. It would be picked up and passed on in our sewers.

'It is quite awful to contemplate. But today, in a war-ravaged Europe, with large groups of men cheek-by-jowl – it doesn't matter which side they are on – it would spread to millions in a matter of weeks. Plague knows no frontiers . . . has no politics.'

The doctor had started to attend to Shaw's leg. 'Get him on the bed in there . . . I can take the bullet out quite easily, I think, and there is some antiseptic in my case . . . and bring one two-inch bandage.'

They shifted Shaw onto the palliasse in the other room. Monique stayed behind, seemingly unable to connect or get herself together. The lean-faced Girton also stayed to question.

'What are our chances of survival, Pascal? Please, we all deserve the truth.'

'Not very high, I'm afraid. We have all been exposed. Several of us may already be infected. I would say . . . twenty per cent is a reasonable figure, no more.'

Girton took this with equanimity. 'What can we do? There must be something!'

Keldermans rummaged in his Gladstone bag. 'The spreading is primarily pneumonic. Everyone should wear some sort of face-mask – a handkerchief, a piece of lining-material . . . anything. Keep the mouth and nose covered at all times, and change the cloth every four hours. Burn the old ones in the grate. The sick man's mouth will be covered in the same way, whatever his temperature. I will keep it in place with an elastic band. Has anyone got one?'

Two were forthcoming as the old doctor went towards his two patients. There was a sudden fierce and earnest desire to help. It was another manifestation of fear. The sound of ripping cloth indicated that they were all attending to their masks as Keldermans sat on the bed and attended to the bullet wound. His face showed his sorrow and apology, and Shaw had settled down to acceptance, not without a touch of shame for his panic. He gritted his teeth desperately as Keldermans removed the bullet from the fleshy part of the leg with forceps, and for a moment passed into half-consciousness from which he was roused by the short sharp sting of bismuth powder and the tightening of a bandage round the leg. The bleeding was minimal and Shaw gasped out his tension slowly before looking up into the doctor's face.

'Sorry, doctor, I just panicked. I'm all right now.'

Keldermans smiled his kind old smile, and nodded without speaking, then turned his attention once more to the fever-wracked body of McQuaig.

Monique came to him again, her face showing the strain of the desperate situation in which she found herself. Lifeline was *her* responsibility now – not Albert's, not anyone's – it was hers and she was responsible for something like two hundred-and-thirty lives, plus whatever the total of evaders might be at that moment.

'Pascal, couldn't you go and find some medicines? There has to be something!'

He turned his grey head to her and tried to speak calmly and kindly. 'It only takes *one* carrier, my dear. In any event there is nothing I can give them. I have had no sulphonamides for the last six months. Isolation is what matters. Then disposal.'

'But I have things to do! There is the line. There's the restaurant. I have to go and see Albert tomorrow, I just can't sit here!'

'You will have to. There is no other way. I meant what I said about using the gun . . . even on you, my dear.'

As if unwilling to pursue that line of thought he turned to the others. 'Shall we all try and conserve our energies. Keep talking down to the minimum. Sleep if you can. We will know in a day or so how many of us are infected. Has anyone had any hospital experience?'

One of the R.A.F. gunners, short with curly hair, stood up. 'I was an orderly for three months once, before I joined up.'

Keldermans accepted the offer with alacrity and organised a rota of simple chores, both domestic and medical. After a few hours they all settled down to a long, tense waiting. Monique kept herself apart from the rest, sitting with her back against the wall of the room and staring at the floorboards. It became very silent with only the sound of McQuaig's choked breathing.

The doctor took his ease near to her and tried to doze without success.

At last she spoke, little more than a whisper. 'What about the men who brought him here? Won't they be infected?'

'It's possible. The incubation period might just by-pass them. But there is nothing we can do about it, is there? My guess is that the collectors are probably safe.'

'My God! I hope so.'

Then one of the other evaders made a quick bolt for the cracked and stained lavatory pan, and was heard to vomit and retch.

Kessler probed into the back of the drawer of Reinhardt's desk. Nothing else of significance. He removed the single manilla file and opened it on the desk, accidently knocking over the silver Luftwaffe-symbol paper-weight on the desk blotter. Kessler already knew there were no personal things on or in Reinhardt's desk. No family photos, no precious mementoes. Reinhardt seemed to have no background, no 'other' life. Gestapo checks had discovered that there was no immediate family, no wife, no child. Reinhardt had been orphaned in the First World War while still a small child and had been brought up by an uncle in a village south of Lubeck. That uncle was now dead. There was no one.

The file contained mostly notes, diagrams, doodles with lists of references for other file consultations. There were also carbon copies of pages from his predecessor's files. Major Brandt had been meticulous in recording every movement he made, with footnotes concerning their relevance or implication. Reinhardt's blue pencil markings on these copies were instructive but inconclusive.

'Have you lost something, Sturmbannfuhrer?'

Kessler stopped rifling the papers and looked up, quite unperturbed that he had been caught red-handed in another officer's desk, assuming that with Reinhardt out in the field he would have a chance to investigate surreptitiously what he could not legitimately obtain without elaborate procedure and red-tape.

Reinhardt threw his cap onto the corner chair and advanced to the desk. His boots showed that he had been scrambling about in the mud and several burrs clung to the legs of his breeches.

'It is not what is *in* the file, Kessler, it is putting two-and-two together and making five.'

'I was interested to see how you were progressing, that is all. Well, did you find anything?'

'Crashed planes, hidden folded parachutes, tyre tracks. The usual. Ah, yes, and this . . . ' He threw a sweet packet to Kessler, plain white paper clearly containing some sticky mess as if straight from a schoolboy's overstuffed pocket.

Kessler peered inside, and wrinkled his nose in distaste. 'What on earth is it?'

'Fresh dates. I found them on the floor of a B.17 with the Navigator's things. It implies that I was right. They are flying from North Africa. Try one, they're very good.'

He helped himself from the bag that Kessler was holding as if it were a bomb about to explode.

The SS officer threw the bag onto the table with an exclamation of disgust. 'So. Another abortive sortie!'

Reinhardt smiled. 'I don't think so. I haven't had a fresh date since I was in the Caucasus.'

Kessler stood up with irritation. 'Your facetiousness does you no credit, Major. If things were different I might choose to reprimand you.'

'Reprimand away, Kessler. You don't frighten me.'

Kessler looked at him with that peculiarly albino look, and narrowed his eyes as he hissed, 'I can have you skinned alive, Reinhardt. Don't ever forget it. The SS have powers overruling anything you might try to hide behind.'

Reinhardt's eyes glinted dangerously as he stood up angrily. 'I know those powers, Kessler. Europe is littered with such obscenities.'

Kessler slapped his hand down on the desk as if to silence him, then walked quickly round the desk and out of the Luftwaffe office slamming the door behind him.

Reinhardt sighed and blew out his cheeks, then tossed the sticky date packet onto his desk top. 'That, as Clauswitz said, is the Death Wish. Nothing if not German!'

Natalie found the side door locked when she arrived back at the Candide. She fumbled for her own key – one which she was allowed now that she was living there during Albert's imprisonment. Inside the place was dark and silent. She called out. 'Monique! Monique!'

There was no answer. Nothing stirred. Quickly she went into the backroom and switched on the light, then through behind the bar where the restaurant switch-panel was, and threw four switches. The resultant illumination only confirmed that the place was deserted, and nothing had been done to prepare for the evening opening. She ran upstairs to the bedrooms. There, too, it was silent and empty of life. She heard a sound downstairs, and called out again for Monique, as she tripped down the narrow staircase. But it was only Justine, looking anxious and frightened.

'Where is everyone, Justine? Monique should have been back hours ago.'

But Justine knew nothing. She had come to work at the usual time to find Pierre, the cook, and Sabine, the kitchen-helper both standing outside unable to gain access to their place of employment. After an hour they had gone home. When something was 'wrong' you did not stay to find out what or why. Not these days. You got lost quickly and silently.

'Justine, go and get them back quickly. We must open this evening, just the same. Hurry. I will get the place ready and do what I can . . .'

It was then that Alain Muny arrived carrying his boxes of vegetables. 'What the hell's going on? I've been back twice already.' Then he saw the worried look in Natalie's eyes. 'Something happened, love?'

'I don't know, Alain. Monique should have been back hours ago. Will you ring Bastien and see if he can tell you anything?'

She set about laying the tables and setting the cutlery while Alain went into the office and used the telephone as circumspectly as he could. She was setting the last napkins when he returned grim-faced.

'No one knows anything. She hadn't arrived. No one has seen her or the children.' He scratched his chin. 'Something's funny here. I tried Doctor Keldermans to see if he had been to give them a check-up. He's not there either, and they expected him back hours ago.'

Natalie looked at him and made the necessary decision without faltering. 'You'd better ring Security headquarters. Do it now. Willi comes off duty in ten minutes time. We have to, Alain. We must know.'

Willi de Hooch, a Flemish accounts-clerk with a suitable political background that he had carefully invented, was their contact within the lion's den, security H.Q. itself. The building on the Avenue Louise housed both the Gestapo and the Luftwaffe Polizei and employed more than twenty Belgian clerking personnel of approved attitudes. Willi had been there three years and had fed Lifeline information whenever it was required. He had taken apalling risks and come through unscathed – so far. He would know if any of their people were being held. His answer, when it came, was negative. There were no Lifeline people being held, nor were there any evaders in the basement cells being 'processed'.

'Then what can have happened? Where are they?' said Natalie. Alain decided to ask around, and set off on his push-bike to do the cafés and bars.

It was Shaw who asked for the light to be put out for a while. He was now in fever and retching regularly. His face and neck had taken on the awful scarlet of inflammation, and he perspired unmercifully. Early that evening one of the others, Colin, a Flight Sergeant Bomb-Aimer who had been quiet but appeared to be merely feeling off-colour had suddenly made a dash for the lavatory, and had been found there fifteen minutes later quite dead. McQuaig still fought back but was weakening rapidly.

Now it was Shaw, and the pain in his leg from the bullet wound was now sharp and burning, and he sensed there was a suppuration spreading into the bandage muslin that had more to do with the fever than the new wound.

The following morning was overcast and it drizzled for the first few hours of daylight. Albert stood on the chair of his cell and looked out across the courtyard. Why didn't they have a clock-tower? Why couldn't there be a clock in the corridor outside the cells? It was important for an inmate to know the time, on visiting-days. Other days it didn't matter. Better, almost, if one was unaware of the slow progress of the days, the weeks, the months.

One corner of the yard was lower than the rest and water was gathering into puddles that reflected the greyness of the day. Albert stepped down, replaced his chair and walked to the cell door and pounded upon it. 'Gavin! Gavin!'

After a moment the warder slipped open the Judas hole. 'What d'you want?'

'Jacques . . . what time is it?'

'I can't come to every cell just to tell someone the time.'

'It's visiting-day. Why have I not been sent down?'

The visiting-hours had been changed to mornings from the customary afternoon sessions usual in most parts of the world that permitted prison visiting. Why no one knew. It was just the German way – being difficult because they decided it was to be that way.

'No one's asked for you, Albert. It's ten to twelve now. No one's coming.'

'But there *has* to be! It's the seventh of August . . . It's "Visiting" !'

Jacques Gavain was not sadist enough to rub a prisoner's nose in his predicament. He felt sorry for most of his charges, and he knew Albert Foiret. He had often been a patron at the old Café Candide before Albert went up in the world and became a restaurateur. He looked sympathetically at his prisoner. 'Sorry, Albert. Not this time.'

Albert turned away and walked back to his chair and flopped down onto it, then got up and lay on his bunk bed. He wanted to cry. Like a runaway child he missed his home and his loved ones. He missed Monique, and he was scared.

Alain went from café to café, visited all the known haunts and contacted most of the Brussels evasion-line personnel known to him. That wasn't all that many, for evasion-line security was more than good – it was necessarily superb. He got on his bike again and made for the Scharbeek reseau of the local resistance, two of whom he knew from years back. They might know something.

As the sun went down on yet another day, and two more young men in their prime were laid out in the second room, covered with sacking or old newspaper, the depression reached its lowest ebb. Monique had made coffee once more. There wasn't all that much else to do. They had run out of food supplies and there was perhaps enough ersatz coffee for one more brew. She handed mugs to Doctor Keldermans and Girton – mugs that were, by virtue of the first round of drinks, their own. No one else drank from anyone else's mug, nor would ever do so.

'I feel unclean . . . you know?' she said. 'If I ever get out of here I shall scrub my skin till it is raw, and wash twenty times a day. Urgh!'

'Please replace your mask, Monique. Don't take it off or let it slip, even for a minute.' Keldermans sighed loudly and with a great feeling of personal exhaustion. 'I am so tired. Still, it is better than I had dared hope. Only four so far. The others seem to be holding their own. Our carrier – the American – is tough, isn't he. By rights he should have gone first, but he will die in the end. There is no way he can escape that fate, I'm sorry to say.' He paused. 'There is, however, one more victim.'

Girton and Monique looked up questioningly. 'Who is that?'

'Myself.' They gasped at the revelation. 'Doctors are not immune, you know. That is a myth fostered by the American cinema. I'm afraid it is true. I can feel the bubo coming in my groin and I have all the other symptoms coming up in text-book fashion. I somehow never thought I would ever see plague, let alone experience it first-hand.'

Monique started to cry softly. 'Pascal, what are we going to do? It's worse than anything I could imagine. It's a nightmare!'

Girton was more positive. 'Can't we risk it, sir? We haven't a hope in hell without you.'

'You have exactly the same chances with or without me, I can assure you. What is your name? We didn't have a chance to become acquainted.'

'Girton, sir. Adam Girton. Flight-Sergeant.'

'Well, Adam. I've been sitting here thinking that I have to hand over the reins to someone – and the gun. There are also instructions for getting rid of everything which I must impart to someone. It rather looks as if you are elected.'

He turned to Monique sadly. 'It isn't that I think you are not up to it, my dear. But it is quite likely that things might happen . . . things you would be forced to do that I would rather spare you.'

'I hope I can do the job.' Girton bit his teeth and looked at them both with misgiving. Keldermans rounded on him with a fierceness and vehemence that startled them both.

'You have to! You must understand that, you *have* to control it! There is something else I have come to realise while sitting here.' He gave a weary chuckle. 'There are always permutations.'

'No, there can't be anything else. There can't be!' There was plea in Monique's voice as well as expostulation, but the old doctor brushed it aside.

'I'm afraid there is, my dear. Such an outbreak as plague is so highly unlikely that there is every possibility, should it spread outside, that one side or the other will convince itself that the epidemic is no accident.'

He let this shocking realisation take its full effect in the ensuing silence.

Monique lifted puzzled eyes over her yashmak-like mask. 'I don't understand.'

But Girton did. He was grimly awed as he spoke. 'I do. You mean that either the Allies or the Germans will think it is the result of deliberate germ warfare.'

'Yes. It would be such an easy and obvious conclusion.'

'And it would provoke retaliation. My God! It doesn't bear thinking about.'

'That is why *no one* must leave this room unless they are without infection. You must burn them . . . completely. Clothing, everything. Nothing is to remain. Anyone who survives will have to get petrol or paraffin from somewhere and start the pyre. In this room would be the best.'

They stared at each other fearfully, trying not to visualise the future.

Then Wade spoke up. 'Hey! Sh . . . sh! There's somebody outside on the stairs.'

Monique took off her shoes and tiptoed across the floor swiftly, holding her ear against the wood. There was no doubt about it. Someone was approaching with stealth up the last few stairs, crossing the landing and stopping outside their door. She held her breath.

'Monique? Pascal?'

It was the whispered voice of Alain, and a sudden leap of hope jumped inside her chest.

'Alain!' This time it was no whisper. It was a cry of anguish, and it came out with all the frightened power of her lungs. 'Alain!'

Outside on the landing a wary and grim-faced Alain heard the cry and went to the door, tried the handle and found it locked. 'Monique! Open the door, girl . . . What's going on?'

'Alain . . . listen, please. Pascal and I are here with the children . . . Alain, we have plague.'

Alain didn't seem to hear or understand. 'Come on, luv. Open the door. We can't talk this way . . . '

It was at that moment that with a superhuman effort Doctor Keldermans staggered across the hall and fell against the door, his face already red in patches. When he spoke it was with unequivocal urgency and authority.

'Listen to me, Alain, carefully. Everyone in this apartment is infected with bubonic plague – the Black Death. It is so serious that no one may come out until it is over. If there is anyone left.' He was suddenly wracked with a bout of coughing, and it was a moment before he could continue.

'If no one comes out in two days time you are to pour petrol under the door or throw the can into the room and set fire to it immediately. I mean that! The room key should be on the floor by your feet.'

Alain glanced down and spotted the simple mortise-lock key. He stared at it without bending down, his mind dazed and not quite grasping what he had been told. His instinct was to think someone was pulling his leg, but not the old man, not Pascal Keldermans.

'But, I don't . . . ' He stopped and frowned. 'Is there nothing I can get? Something from the surgery? Shouldn't I alert the civil authorities?'

'No!' The old man's voice was urgent and pleading. 'Please accept what I say, Alain. This is very, very serious.' A moment, then. 'I want you to go and get a drum of petrol.'

'There isn't any petrol – anywhere.'

Alain was speaking no more than the truth. There had been no petrol, ration or blackmarket, for weeks now. Rumour had it that the Germans were themselves almost without. Again it was the aged doctor who spoke.

'Yes, there is. In the big garage behind my house you will find my ambulance. Inside the ambulance you will find a drum full of refined gasoline. I have had it since 1941. You must bring it here, somehow. On second thoughts I think you must tell Inspector Delon – no one else – and he can have the fire-brigade standing by on some excuse. You *must* let the whole floor burn thoroughly.'

'I can't just do that, Pascal . . . '

'You *have* to! There is no alternative the way we are placed. If anyone survives, and there should be one or two, they must be got into isolation wards in the Sacre Coeur. Nowhere else! We can trust the sisters. One last thing – could you bring us some food? I don't think anyone feels like it now, but we must have something.'

Alain stooped to pick up the key and turned to leave. As his footfall echoed within the deserted house his mind was racing, as well as trying to recover and accept.

Reinhardt sat at his desk facing the two young officers before him. Both were under seventeen years of age and their pale beardless chins testified to that immaturity.

'So. You have been posted. I am sorry we did not have time to get to know each other better. May I know where you have been posted?'

'Kastort, sir. Both of us.'

'Ah, yes. The defence of the Fatherland is now the only priority. You will be able to run into Lübeck when you are off-duty. I envy you.'

The younger of the two frowned and looked at him with his pale blue eyes. 'How will you manage, sir? There are so few . . . '

'What we do now is of no importance. It is in your hands now. Have you seen to your men?'

From the blank reaction the veteran knew that his youngsters had not done so. Probably too taken up with their own problems to do anything more than issue a curt command to an N.C.O. He sighed.

'Always look after your men, Karl. They come first. Do not leave it to your N.C.O.s. They are good men, and they are disheartened. They *need* you. Look after them.'

Karl Ruschke, Leutnant of three weeks, bowed his head in shame, but there was no anger in Reinhardt's farewell as he shook hands.

'Good luck. I doubt if we will meet again.'

The door opened as they turned to go. Kessler entered and regarded them critically, and returned their formal salute. Once they had gone he turned to Reinhardt, removed his cap and wiped the band. The day was hot.

'Your men are leaving, I see. Well, the Fatherland needs them.'

Reinhardt saw fit not to reply. What was the point? There is no answer to such fatuousness.

Kessler continued. 'I have been recalled to Berlin for a few days. In regard to Lifeline, you implied that your searches were bearing fruit. I am delighted, of course, but the Gestapo will need a little more than vague promises, Herr Major.'

'Anyone who has served on the Russian front puts little faith in vague promises, Sturmbannfuhrer. We had our fill of those. You will find no shortage of them in Berlin. I have pursued several of Brandt's leads. He was right. I know he was, and *he* knew he was. For some reason he did not follow them through.'

Kessler's lip curled. 'We have already covered this ground, Major. It is still no more than speculation.'

'If that is how you regard it, then, yes.'

Kessler turned on his heel and swept out without another word. Reinhardt watched him go. Their surface working relationship was wearing thin, and Reinhardt knew that one day – perhaps not far way – Kessler would make his move against him. He had failed to implicate him in the Hitler Bomb Plot of July, despite many attempts to do so. Reinhardt knew the only thing saving him was the fact that he was – and was known as – an 'ace' flyer, personally decorated by the Fuhrer and publicised in the German press. The people did not take kindly to their heroes being executed as 'traitors'. But one day . . .

In the stifling and stinking apartment, its decay and dilapidation now enhanced by pestilence, the survivors waited for the end in silence. Only the coughing and retching was heard from time to time, and now they were all oblivious to those sounds.

Girton, still apparently unaffected, ministered to the old doctor. The young man sensed the gravity of his own position but he was also aware that Doctor Keldermans was not succumbing as readily as the others. His age and constitution affected him, though his actual infection seemed to be held. He walked down the narrow hall towards the kitchen where the coffee-pot stood on the ancient cooker. He realised there was no more ersatz coffe, but it might be worthwhile to boil up the grounds again – for the third time.

Then he stopped in his tracks. He had caught a sound from outside and moved as silently as possible to the door and applied his ear to the panel.

Monique had heard the sound, too, and was standing in the room doorway staring at the lock.

'Pascal! Monique!'

It was Alain's voice.

Outside on the landing Alain lowered the drum of petrol onto the floor at the side of the door. Behind him, on the top step of the broken stairway, Natalie stood wide-eyed and pale and stared at the entrance. She was clutching a small bag of sacking.

Girton put the pistol back into his belt and sighed with relief.

Monique rushed to the door. 'Alain?'

But it was Natalie's voice she heard as the younger girl hurried to the other side of the wood. 'Monique!'

Alain spoke again, firmly and without emotion. 'The petrol's outside here. There aren't many Germans about now, so it wasn't any problem getting here. I've filled a couple of bottles and plugged them with a wick. Straight "Molotovs", in case you need 'em.'

'Did you speak with Delon?'

'He's waiting for my call. Where's Pascal?'

'He's ill. Not as bad as the others, I think, but too bad to come here.'

Natalie spoke up, trying to steady her voice. 'I got you some medicines. It's German stuff. I thought it might help. Sulphonamides. Will that help?'

There was a scuffling sound before Monique's voice replied, 'Pascal says "wonderful". What did you have to give for them?'

Alain chuckled malevolently. 'Belgian civilian papers. That's all the Germans want these days. There's some food as well.'

It was Girton's voice who spoke next. 'Can he push them through the door if I open it, and stand back . . . '

'I heard that. We'll leave them in the doorway and cover our faces and stand back. It'll be all right.'

Inside they heard the thud of the drum, followed by the soft drag of sacking on floorboards. Then footsteps, and a muffled voice saying, 'I'm turning the key . . . now.'

The evaders who could move were all gathered across the entrance hall to watch the key turning in the lock and there was a sharp intake of breath as the door opened slightly. Through that opening, as it widened, the imprisoned wretches saw the figures of Natalie and Alain crouching against the rear wall, wide-eyed and holding handkerchiefs to their faces. In the doorway was the petrol drum and bulging sack.

Suddenly, with a cry both mad and triumphant, the American McQuaig hurtled past them through the door, knocked over the gasoline drum and thundered down the stairs.

Monique screamed out, 'No-o!'

Keldermans shouted, 'Stop him, at all costs stop him.'

Girton threw the Walther pistol towards Alain as the latter jumped forward and grabbed the two 'Molotov cocktails' and stuffed them into his jacket pocket, then set off after Natalie who was clattering down the stairs in hot pursuit of the American. The flyer had somehow found the energy and control of his limbs to stagger out in that one sudden burst of frightened energy.

Alain yelled after her, 'Don't lose him! Whatever you do don't lose him!'

No one had thought for the Germans, for any mundane security. This was basic and desperate, and they knew it. That American who was carrying the most appalling infection known to man had to be stopped at any cost. They leapt and clattered down the stairwell as they heard the front door thrown open and bang against the peeling wall. Then the footsteps were gone.

Already finding his sudden-found energy spent, McQuaig staggered and tripped into the street. His vision was blurred and the blood was pounding inside his head. A trickle of blood came from one ear and soaked into the shirt collar as he moved across the street and took the first turning amid the abandoned buildings of the quarter.

It was not a forbidden area. There was no cordon, no barrier, but few people ever came here. No one lived or worked here. Only the disused gasworks soared behind the crumbling houses, and half of the streets led nowhere. It was the end of the line for most things. Cul-de-sac after blind alley.

But McQuaig had disappeared by the time Natalie reached the daylight of the street. There was even little of that, as dusk was spreading across the metropolis. A blacked-out capital does not make itself felt in the same way as a thriving, illumined city of peace. In the dirt-filled purple sky, broken with the plumes of factory smoke and slashed by the dirty yellow streaks of setting sun, there was only a sense of an uninhabited, devastated planet. Alain stood stock-still and listened for any clue. It came almost immediately as McQuaig fell against a wooden board that dropped to the pavement with a thud like a distant gun shot. They set off immediately in the direction of the sound.

As if in response to their own footfall, they heard the clatter of boots preceeding them, then suddenly fall silent.

Both stopped, waited, then continued on silent feet towards the source of the last sound. Around them the empty windows, unglazed or shattered, stared at them. Doors, boarded and blistered, rejected any advance.

From a nearby railway sidings an engine chinked and clunked.

They turned into the final cul-de-sac. There was only one alley at the far end, by the tarred and blistered sleepers that formed the containing walls. A small shunting-engine was heard approaching and suddenly the whole alley was engulfed in steam and smoke as it passed under the nearby iron bridge on the fringe of the gasworks area.

Alain chucked the pistol to Natalie and grabbed a wooden spile about the size of a pick-handle. Together they moved into the bottle-neck. With a snarl and a last-effort leap McQuaig jumped out into the alley from the doorway in which he was shadowed and moved towards them. Natalie gritted her teeth and fired two shots into him. As he fell he turned his rabid-looking face to stare at them. There was fear and bewilderment in his eyes – with a huge roseate patch of suppurating sore beneath. Natalie felt sick and turned away, dropping the gun on the cobbles.

Alain slowly took the Molotovs from his jacket and placed them on the ground at his feet, before he turned to Natalie, who was sobbing, her head against the crumbling brick wall.

'Be better if you went, love. I'll do what has to be done. Go on.'

Natalie nodded, refused to look round again, and walked stumblingly away, round the corner, and down the alley. Alain waited until he could not hear her footfall, then turned back and took matches from his pocket, lit one of the Molotov wicks, held it at arm's length and looked at the still body of the American flyer.

'Sorry, old son. It's the only way.'

He threw the bottle so that it smashed by the side of the dead man. It burst into flame with a roar. The petrol that had fallen on the clothing caught immediately as the flame spread across the cobbles and engulfed the body. Alain grimly threw the second bottle into it. With a whoosh and a muffled boom the pyre increased.

The shunter passed again under the iron bridge and the cul-de-sac was again immersed in smoke which seemed to turn the fumes from the pyre black. Alain turned away. He felt sicker than he had done since the war started.

It was the middle of the following week that Monique was released from the Sacre Coeur. She was lucky and had escaped infection totally. Pascal Keldermans recovered more slowly. He, too, survived without after-effect. At least without physical effect. Everyone who had survived that episode was mentally scarred. Inspector Delon had arranged a splendid exercise for the Fire Brigade, ensuring that the whole block was totally engulfed in flame before permitting the services to engage in any fire-fighting. He had obtained permission from both the City Fathers and the German Kommandant. Both considered that, in view of the Allied advance, such practise could only be a responsible precaution, and he was complimented for the thoroughness of his preparations.

But the danger moment arrived when Major Reinhardt turned up at the Candide the same evening that Monique was again appearing. He was curious to find out if she would tell the same story – about her mother's illness – that had been the reason given by Natalie for her wonted absence.

'I trust your mother is properly recovered, Mademoiselle?'

Something about the tone of voice put Monique immediately on her guard and she improvised round the truth as she explained. 'Thank you, Herr Major, she is now well. Actually it is not my real mother – as I am sure you are already aware. The lady who brought me up after my mother's death I always call "Maman", but she is not related in any way. But I love her and owe her so much.'

Reinhardt smiled at her – whether because he was glad she had not fallen into his trap, or because he was appreciative of an expert liar was not clear. She returned to the back room. 'Be careful of that one, Natalie. He is closer than he knows.'

The following morning she visited Albert in the Havenlaan prison. Albert was already champing in the interview room when she was shown in and went to her place.

'Where the hell have you been? You were supposed to be here last week. Nobody came. Doesn't anyone care about me any longer?'

'We all care, Albert. Things needed doing, that was all.'

Albert calmed down having got the anger off his chest. He was aware enough to know that such things happen and he could not expect anyone to put him before their duty to the evaders. 'Anything serious?'

'No. We had a small problem. It's all settled now. Natalie is well and sends her love, as does Alain and Pascal.'

'Pascal said he would try and visit. How is he?'

'He is still in hospital, actually . . . '

'Hospital!'

'He's going to be all right. He picked up an infection from one of his patients. Nothing to worry about . . . '

AUGUST 1944

As the summer wore on the Allies consolidated their hold on Normandy and northern France. By the end of August the Germans were in full retreat to the north and the east, but Hitler's much vaunted 'secret weapons' were beginning to emerge. It is fascinating to realise that most of today's advanced weaponry was already well beyond the drawing-board stage. Even the nuclear bomb that burst upon the world at Hiroshima the following year was well advanced within the Third Reich. However, the weapons that were plunged into immediate service were the V-1 flying bombs, known to the British on whom they fell in considerable quantity as 'doodle-bugs'. They caused relatively slight damage and were rapidly shot down, and Britain learned not only to live with them, but to treat them with the disdain they probably deserved. But the V-2, virtually an intercontinental missile, was a different thing altogether. Had Hitler managed to perfect and mass-produce this rocket at a slightly earlier stage in the war the outcome could well have been different, and it is perfectly conceivable that Germany could now be dominating not only Europe, including the United Kingdom, but the whole U.S.S.R., the Far East, and the continent of America. Fate was kind to us. Time was against him.

After the fall of Paris it was relatively easy for agents to be sent into Belgium and the Low Countries with the avowed purpose of sabotaging the experimental firings of the V-2 rockets. The German stockpile of rockets at that time was in the region of 1,800. Within weeks that number rose alarmingly, and by the end of the war some

10,000 had been produced, if not fired. They were one of the greatest threats to the Allies that the Germans came up with.

Among the several agents sent into Belgium was Major Nick Bradley, of SOE. They chose him because he knew the rockets (having been in Peenemunde in the developing days) and he had worked with Lifeline on one occasion in 1943. They knew him, therefore, and would accept him more easily. It was only shortly before he was to make his way through the German lines into Belgium that Bradley was given a second mission to add to his already difficult job. London had learned that Albert Foiret had been imprisoned by the Civil Authorities and that Mademoiselle Duchamps was therefore running Lifeline. Bradley was to ensure that all was well, that no other evaders were to be sent down any route but secreted somewhere in the Ardennes or the Biesbosch until such time as they could join up with the Allied advance.

His first job was not going to be easy, but the second might prove even more problematic if the Belgians, naturally enough, resented any interference of their sovereignty by London. It would take tact – not one of Bradley's strong points.

His initial contact proved more amenable than he had expected. There was resentment at first, but it wore down, and they tolerated his presence at the same time as they welcomed his expertise.

Kessler returned from Berlin promoted to the rank of Standartenfuhrer.

The mills of justice were grinding slower than Albert or Guissard had hoped, largely due to the war situation, for no one knew what was happening. The Allies drew closer and the Germans started to leave the capital, but still, anyone overstepping the rigid bounds of curfew, and anything the Germans considered to be opposition, was dealt with summarily. That was intimidating to the judiciary as well as anyone else. So Albert continued to languish in the Havenlaan prison.

3

Just Light the Blue Touch Paper

Natalie stepped into the restaurant and crossed to where Monique was waiting for her to report. 'There's no doubt about it. I am being followed.'

Monique turned to Alain. 'And you said you thought I was being followed yesterday?'

'That's right. I didn't spot anyone, but it's a sixth sense you get after a bit.' He turned to Natalie. 'Where did you leave him?'

Bradley moved to the bar. 'If you feel it, the chances are you are right. Show me.'

Natalie crossed to the window overlooking the square. Most of the glass was textured, to fit the external appearance of the Grand' Place, but there was one panel almost free of rippling, and it was possible to make out most of the exterior through it.

'Look! That's him, the one with the fair hair and the newspaper.'

Bradley said nothing but took it in thoroughly before he turned back to the group. The moment Alain mentioned he thought Monique was being tailed Bradley had called them all together to discuss the situation and decide upon a course of action. It could mean nothing more than a check-out from some vague report. It could mean they were now the objects of scrutiny by the Gestapo. It could mean their days were numbered. Bradley looked at Keldermans.

'What about you, doctor?'

'I can't say that I have noticed anything. I am an old man,

Major. My senses aren't as keen as they once were.'

'Did you walk here?'

'Of course. I haven't any petrol. My shoes are wearing thin, and I can't replace them either . . . '

'Right. Would you walk back to your surgery. I want to check something.'

Keldermans nodded and took his hat. He left quietly and without any fuss as Bradley went again to the clear pane in the window and watched.

'Your bloke isn't interested. That means he's after *you* only. Ahah! I retract that. Alain, you got your bike?'

Alain nodded.

'You go down to the Bourse and see if you can buy me some fags. I really have run out.' He immediately went back to the pane and watched the German tails as Alain went out of the side door. They merely glanced at him.

'Number two has gone after the doctor. They don't seem interested in Alain. How often does he come here?'

'Two or three times a week. Sometimes more, sometimes less. Usually in the morning. He delivers vegetables, quite legitimately, unless there is something on.'

'He could be the only one they accept as genuine.' Bradley peered again, then walked back slowly into the room and picked up his brandy.

Monique didn't like him much, but she recognised a true professional when she saw one. 'D'you think they're on to us?'

It was Natalie who replied. 'If they thought they had something concrete they would have rounded us up before now.'

Bradley nodded. 'Right. No, they're just sniffing. When do you see Albert?'

Monique bristled immediately. 'Wednesday. Why?'

'I think he should know. He probably had a plan for such an eventuality . . . '

Monique cut across him. 'No. Albert is out of this. He's staying out of it. I don't intend to worry him.'

'You mean you don't want him to think you can't handle it? Can you handle it?'

'Enough to keep us in operation.'

Bradley eyed her dead-pan. 'You'd better mean just that. We *are* staying in operation – whatever. It is *now* they need us, and it has to be *now* we operate.'

Monique did not like Bradley for assuming. She did not like him because he had a tendency to give orders. And she did not like him because he was the sort of man he was. But London had sent him – for what reason he knew best, and they had been asked to co-operate.

In the Havenlaan prison an interview cell was set aside for prisoners not yet tried to meet their lawyers. It wasn't much of a place. Two chairs and a deal table, but at least they had privacy. The advocate, Maitre Guissard, was already sitting waiting, eyes closed as if in meditation, his fingers interlaced upon his belly. The sound of approaching footsteps suggested that his client was about to come before him. The locks ground and snapped, and keys jangled.

Guissard slipped the watch from his waistcoat pocket and checked the time as Albert Foiret was permitted to enter the interview room and the door slammed shut behind him. They shook hands silently, and Albert sat with the quiet assured mien that is part of the professionalism of business men.

'Well, Guissard?'

'I take it that you are in reasonable health still.'

But Albert would have no pleasantries. 'The Candide, man!'

Guissard looked at him then smiled tightly. 'Bon! The business prospers. Mademoiselle Duchamps says that you are to know that the take remains constant, despite fewer occupying troops. She intends bringing a statement of account with her next Wednesday.'

'And the case? When do I get out?'

'Not so fast, M'sieur Foiret. The mills of justice, you understand . . . '

'Damn it, man. Spare me your turns of phrase. What is happening?'

'They have no real case, M'sieur, as I told you. It remains

entirely circumstantial, based upon gossip and hearsay, larded with envy. Unhappily there were no witnesses to your late wife's death other than Mademoiselle Duchamps, who is, alas, an interested party. Little credence would be given to her testimony. I am therefore applying to the German authorities for their military report upon the incident. They were, you tell me, present at the time of death.'

'My wife slipped and fell down the narrow stairs. She burst through the curtain. Her neck was broken.'

'Quite so. Er, M'sieur Foiret, is there any reason why you would *not* wish me to bring the matter to the attention of the German authorities by asking for access to their civil files?'

Albert hesitated and his mind ran at top speed, clicking through data with the speed and certainty of a computer, Guissard read the hesitation and warned. 'Consider well, my friend, but I would remind you that it is necessary for you to prove your innocence. The onus is not upon the prosecution to prove your guilt.'

Albert waited until his mind had drawn a blank, then shook his head.

Guissard beamed. 'Bon. Then I think we may say you will be out of here within two weeks.'

'I must be out of here before the Allies reach Brussels. It is essential!'

Guissard was in no doubt that Albert meant this last. There was an earnestness in his voice the advocate had not encountered as yet. He suspected, of course, that Albert was much more than merely a black-market restaurateur. He also suspected that Albert was the victim of a plot to have him put out of the way. He did not know that as the Allied armies approached the capital the danger to the members of Lifeline grew more acute. Once the Germans had left the city the tardy patriots would hasten to prove their allegiances and would almost certainly turn upon anyone suspected of collaboration, and Albert could not bear to consider the possible consequences to Monique, Natalie, and the others. No one would believe they were anything other than collaborators, and he was in terror at the possible consequences. Back in his own cell he went over, again and again, how he would need to contact the British special agents who accompanied the spearheads for exactly that purpose! To credit the apparent collaborators with the truth of their undercover deeds. Time, time! He *had* to get out soon.

The evening was half-way gone when Bradley sauntered down from his room and brazenly walked into the restaurant and seated himself at the best table. Natalie – who secretly liked Bradley and was amused by his effrontery – nudged Monique – who was not amused. She walked across to the table briskly as the main entrance door opened and Kessler took off his coat and hung it on the stand.

'What the hell do you think you're doing?'

'I thought I would come down for dinner this evening. I have to eat somewhere, why not here?'

'You don't pay for your food for one thing! This table is usually taken by German officers.'

Bradley smiled his unsufferable smile. 'I don't mind if they join me. I don't like them much but their table manners are faultless. They may still sit here . . . '

Kessler had reached the table and precluded any further exchange. Monique turned an embarrassed face to him. 'I am sorry, Standartenfuhrer. I was trying to explain to this gentleman that the table is reserved.'

Kessler regarded Bradley with cautious expression.

Bradley bent his head with a perfect Germanic bow. 'Luc de Vriendt.'

Kessler was taken slightly aback by the behaviour, and reacted as a good German should by clicking his heels and bowing his own head.

'Kessler, Standartenfuhrer. SS.'

Bradley beamed. 'You must forgive me. I did not properly understand. A seat for the Standartenfuhrer, quickly!'

Monique obliged, equally taken aback, and Kessler seated himself rather portentously. Bradley immediately sat down facing him, still beaming.

'I am delighted to make your acquaintance, Standartenfuhrer. We know of your work here in Belgium . . . '

Kessler was shaken by Bradley's confidence and sat back uneasily. He was too used to party members simply being 'there' to react without careful thought to a situation he did not anticipate.

'Indeed? May I know exactly who you are, M'n Herr de Vriendt?'

Bradley delved into his pocket and produced his Organisation Todt card and papers, and offered them to Kessler, who glanced quickly and professionally at them, his eyebrows raised slightly. 'I see. Organisation Todt.'

'I am in Brussels for a few days on business.' He leant forward confidingly. 'Connected with our latest secret weapon.'

Kessler responded on cue and bent towards him, anxious for any confidence that Bradley might impart.

Bradley smiled. 'But before we talk, perhaps you would like to order? Ma'mselle!'

Monique stepped forward and waited.

'The Standartenfuhrer will be my guest this evening, and we will start with a bottle of the Montrachet I saw earlier. Is that to your taste, Kessler?'

The SS man beamed, as anyone might invited to share a bottle of Montrachet.

'Montrachet would be a very considerable treat, Bauleiter. Thank you.'

Bradley managed to avoid the look of daggers given him by Monique as she departed to comply with the order. At the bar she gave vent to her feelings to Natalie and fumed, 'That Bradley is insufferable! Imagine . . . taking a table with Kessler and inviting him to join him "on the house".'

Natalie chuckled. 'He's got the cheek of the devil, that one. Maybe that's why he's survived all that he has.'

But Monique was looking for excuses as she thumped a bottle of the wine on the counter top. 'Montrachet, indeed! We've only got four bottles left. Albert paid the earth for them.'

Natalie touched the bottle with the back of her hand.

'It's not cold enough.'

But Monique was determined to get back at Bradley. 'Hard bloody luck!' She thumped the ice-bucket into its stand and crammed the ice into the space round the bottle as Natalie smothered a grin and went to her own tables.

Bradley and Kessler quickly dropped into mutually respectful roles and soon were deep in conversation.

'I spent two years in the Research Laboratories perfecting the long-range arrow-shells. You probably know all about them. Recently they were redeveloped for high-accuracy 105mm Flak guns. They are very accurate, you know, and the velocity is extraordinary,' Bradley paused and glanced about him before proceeding. 'However, I am here now in connection with our latest A-4 rockets. There have been only test-firings so far, and they have caused havoc in England. We are about to launch over a thousand missiles against France and England.'

Kessler was obviously impressed by the confidence, as well as being interested. 'I was naturally aware that this was in progress. Indeed, I have witnessed a demonstration recently from one of the more permanent sites . . . '

'Which one was that?' Bradley made the question sound just interested enough to imply professional concern and Kessler bought it.

'At Zandvliet, not far from Antwerp.'

Bradley dived into his wallet again and produced a small diary. He perused a host of meaningless scrawls with insistence. 'Zandvliet, Zandvliet, ah, yes. I am due to inspect that site on one of its firing-days. Unfortunately no one saw fit to tell me *when* they were. I shall have to apply to the Kommandantur tomorrow morning . . '

Kessler was helpfulness itself. 'You must see Oberstleutnant Wittrich, on the third floor. He will have the details.'

Bradley wrote the name in his diary. 'Wittrisch . . . third floor. I will see him. But I am talking too much. Tell me of your work here. Your name is well known, Standartenfuhrer. You have done great things here in Belgium . . . '

The following morning the two German 'tails' were to be seen hovering in the Grand' Place. They sat outside the café, having moved their tables well out from the sidewalk, drank coffee, and smoked endless foul cigarettes, leaving the litter of stubs around the table legs.

When Natalie came in from the kitchen she found Monique having a go at Bradley.

'It isn't the cost of the wine, it's the way you walk around as if everyone is supposed to follow without question. The way you damn well take everything for granted.'

Bradley merely looked at her with an amused smile playing about his lips. 'And the wine wasn't properly chilled. The ice-bucket is to keep it at a reasonable temperature, not shock it into submission.'

'Never mind the wine! You were skating on very thin ice last night. Kessler is nobody's fool, Major. You would do well not to underestimate him. While you were trying to be clever with him Kessler could just as easily be playing with you. *Avoid* contact wherever possible . . .'

'And how would I get the rocket-site schedules if I didn't ask for them?'

That stopped Monique in her tracks. Both girls looked at Bradley.

'What schedules?'

'We already know half of the sites they are using for their test-launchings, but they are not permanent sites. They move around from one to the other. If we are not going to waste a hell of a lot of time we need to know *when*. I needed to know who had that information. Kessler told me.'

Even Monique looked at him queerly. 'Kessler?'

'He thinks I work for the Todt Organisation in the Peenemunde sites. I did, of course, but not for Germany.'

Both girls knew enough of Bradley's background to know that he spoke less than the truth. He had personally brought out a Polish scientist vital to the Peenemunde project and brought him across Holland into Brussels to wait for transport to the United Kingdom. That was when he first contacted Lifeline, in

1942. But Monique was not about to congratulate him.

'All right, so you've been clever.' But he floored her as he so often did by becoming the supplicant. She had never grasped the simple truth that Bradley respected Lifeline and its members very deeply, and recognised their peculiar merits.

'Now, I need your help. On the third floor of the Kommandantur a certain Oberstleutnant Wittrich has an office. He has the information I need. Who do you have in the Kommandantur?'

Monique was not blind to the fact that Bradley assumed they had a plant inside the headquarters. That presumed he thought them geared to such things.

'Willi de Hooch is a clerk with the civil administration offices. He supplies us with most of our blank documents and keeps us informed of what they are up to. But it won't be easy.'

'It won't be too difficult either. The Germans are packing-up. Half of them went last week. They won't know what is going on. I doubt if they really know who has gone and who hasn't. He can do it, today.'

Monique looked him coldly in the face, knowing him to be right again, and disliking him for it. 'I'll see to it. What else?'

'You said you had a bunch of evaders in a wood somewhere south-east of Antwerp . . . '

'Yes. They bivouac there because we have no room in safe-houses any more, and we can't get them back to England . . . just like the others.'

'They live not too far from where I want to go. Tomorrow we should have the information. Can we go and meet this lot, this afternoon?'

Natalie checked her wristwatch and mentally ran through the train time-table that she knew backwards. 'I can take Major Bradley. There's time.'

'Yes. But you will need special movement-papers. I have some, they just need filling out. They were stamped yesterday.'

Bradley looked at her, trying to catch her eyes directly. 'You see, it can be relatively painless.'

Natalie had crossed to the window and was checking the

tails in their coffee drinking. Bradley was transferring bits and pieces from one jacket to the one he was wearing when she turned round.

'The second one has just gone into the tobacconist across the square. That means no one is watching the side door. Come on. We go now while we have the chance.'

She grabbed her coat and made for the door. Bradley turned to Monique as he passed and smiled widely. 'The name is still Nick. It's quite easy to say. Try it sometime.'

The door closed and Monique sighed to herself, then smiled and turned back to the account books. Albert wanted to know how things stood. She would show him a mere woman could cope just as well as any man. He needed to be reminded and she was about to do just that. Men! They were all the same. Chauvinists.

Natalie and Bradley reached the bivouac area without mishap. Six kilometres outside of Antwerp they dropped from the train, visited a house in the tiny village of Oustrade where a heavy piece of sacking was mutely handed to Bradley. Now they were approaching the area Natalie knew, where she also knew sixty-seven evaders, British and American, were encamped until such time as they could be either moved or could without difficulty rejoin their own lines.

Bradley kept his eyes peeled, in that keen, yet off-hand way he had, as Natalie led him through the wooded scrubland towards the centre of the tree-studded area. Suddenly three men were standing before them, waiting, apparently unarmed, and one actually wearing R.A.F. uniform.

'Saw you coming. We were alerted about eleven, and we've been hanging about since then,' one of the men said.

'Sorry to take so long. We had to call in Oustrade for some equipment,' Natalie answered.

Bradley said nothing, merely nodded smilingly to his escort, who quickly guided them through the undergrowth and the trees to a clearing where what appeared to be a near-prehistoric encampment revealed itself. Gaping dolefully, with foliage camouflage ready to drop into place at a moment's notice, were half-a-dozen 'earths' dug into the ground, like a gargantuan rabbit warren. Close viewing disclosed six fly-sheets, almost invisible to the naked eye, under which basked a dozen or more men, reading, sleeping, or just curiously gawping at the visitors.

Under a poplar-and-beech overhang there was a bleached, mended, and reproofed scout-tent, and standing outside amiably beaming was an R.A.F. officer wearing daubed khaki trousers under a neat R.A.F. battle-top, bearing the insignia of a Wing Commander. Bradley surmised him to be the Senior officer.

He smiled broadly at Natalie and shook her hand with a sense of awkwardness which implied he didn't really know if he ought to kiss it or shake it. 'Hello. Thanks for the grub you had delivered. Got it yesterday. Sixty-odd stomachs say "thank you". We were getting short, and there isn't much game around the marshes.'

'This is Major Bradley of S.O.E.—Wing Commander Newman. He's in charge here.'

The men shook hands and introductions commenced, ending with the uniformed, clean-shaven young man who had met them initially. 'My 2-I-C, Bob Jaclyn. We don't stand on ceremony, here Major. Name's Tony. Take a pew,' said Newman.

They all sat round in a semicircle on the ground as Natalie explained. 'Major Bradley has been sent over by London for a variety of reasons . . . '

Bradley interrupted. 'Natalie, let me do the talking. Okay?' He turned to Newman. 'Wing Commander, Tony, the most important thing I have to do at this moment is knock out as many V-2 sites as I can.'

'Are they the rocket-things?'

'Right. They superseded the doodle-bugs and are making a hell of a mess. If they aren't stopped it *could* make a difference.'

Newman breathed deeply. 'I think I get the picture. Fire-away.'

'They are based in the Low Countries and fired mostly from

mobile sites, usually single launchers. That way we can't bomb the bastards, so it's a job for the blokes on the spot. That's me, and I want it to be "us".'

Jaclyn glanced up at Bradley. 'You want to use some of the chaps as a strike-force. Is that it?'

'Something like that. I mean no disrespect to the R.A.F. but they are untrained in ground hand-combat. I can't afford to carry patsies.'

'We've got quite a few Yanks here. They seem rather good at that sort of thing . . . '

Bradley looked directly at Newman. 'Can you weed-out a small strike-force for me? There's a site in the area that is used frequently. I'm going to have a look at it now. I shall want your bunch the day after tomorrow. Right?'

'You'll have them, Major.'

Bradley stood up and raised an eyebrow to the Wingco. 'Weapons?'

Newman merely nodded, and Bradley continued, 'I want you to hang onto this for me, will you. Treat it gently . . . '

The men shook hands again, and Natalie led Bradley away from the clearing as she gave a parting smile to the men, all beaming like schoolboys at the headmaster's daughter.

Willi de Hooch had worked in the Kommandantur since 1942 when he had been given the choice of transportation to Germany and work in the labour camps, or working for the Third Reich as a 'Greater-Germany volunteer' – for which he would be adequately paid – as a clerk in the Kommandantur. His experience as a local government official was desirable to the new masters, and Willi quickly decided that discretion was the better part of valour and agreed to serve the Burgkommandant in whatever capacity he could.

It was fortunate for Lifeline that he had done so, for once he had been recruited by Albert as his eyes and ears within the enemy citadel Willi had not only done sterling service – he had increased his stature in his own eyes. By nature he was not a courageous man, nor did he have cause to hate his masters the way that many of his countrymen had. It just felt 'right' for him to be a Belgian doing his little bit for Belgium.

He glanced up at the wall-clock. It was three-forty-two, and time he did something about his assignment. He was, of course, terrified, as he was every time he stole papers, or borrowed official stamps, or purloined information at Albert's insistence. He knew it would be slightly easier today because the Germans were preparing for withdrawal. Half of the garrison had already gone, officers were being posted every day, and the first lorry-loads of documents and filing-cabinets had already left for the Fatherland. People were moving about the corridors, offices were in turmoil. It should be reasonably easy, even if it was secret information.

He gathered himself together and left his office to wander down the corridor, round the corner, up the marbled steps. The next floor was no different from his own, general turmoil. He walked past the office door with the tiny card in the brass holder, typed in a faded Gothic script – 'Oberstleutnant Wittrich'.

Willi de Hooch glanced over the top of the frosted panes in the office windows that looked onto the corridor. Inside he could see a pinched, middle-aged woman nervously ploughing through piles of documents and files, the cabinet drawer open behind her. Near her desk a Wehrmacht private, looking no more than fifteen years of age, was packing a tea-chest with selected files. At that moment Oberstleutnant Wittrich came from his inner office and spoke to the woman as he took his cap from the stand. The juvenile private snapped to attention. Wittrich ignored him, picked up his briefcase and gloves, and hurried out into the corridor where Willi de Hooch just happened to be walking.

A moment later Willi entered the Wittrich office with a sense of urgency, out of breath, and requested the already over-wrought lady to give him the rocket-site schedules for the Oberstleutnant who had forgotten them. Without anything but a weary sigh the faded lady disappeared into the inner office, returning a few seconds later with the papers, and handed them to de Hooch.

It was as simple as that. It often was. When it wasn't Willi invented an excuse for Albert saying it was no longer possible or available. Why should he put his life in jeopardy for such things? He could be adequately patriotic in simple things. Enough was enough.

It took Willi no time at all to photograph the relevant material. He had found a disused room behind the caretaker's cubby-hole which he used all the time. Once done, Willi returned the documents to the woman, and made his retreat. There was a one per cent chance that the incident would be mentioned. Good enough odds for Willi de Hooch.

That same day Kessler had left his billet to walk to Security Headquarters. Just before turning into the Avenue Louise he had walked past a large office block down a side street, where someone had tipped a bucketful of slops and filth from the roof or upper-floor directly onto him. He was furious, of course, but realised that he was probably being goaded into finding the culprit where he – alone – would no doubt be dealt with. Resistance and shows of opposition were gradually becoming more overt as the prospect of German evacuation became more likely.

He continued to his office after brushing off as much as he could. There were officers waiting. That sort of thing would now have to be ignored in order to attend to the important matters in hand.

The few remaining officers of any reliability were already assembled waiting. They saw his controlled rage immediately. Reinhardt, standing by the window looking out over the roof tops did not turn until an expostulation from Stroem, the senior of the very young officers left to them made him do so.

'Herr Standartenfuhrer!'

Kessler ignored them all for a moment as he took off his jacket and called for Wullner from the outer office.

'Take this coat and have it cleaned, and fumigated. Now! Clean the cap yourself, as best you can.'

Kessler did not wait till Wullner had picked up the discarded jacket but turned immediately to his junior colleagues.

'Resume your seats.' Then, noting Reinhardt at the window, 'Perhaps you would care to join us, Major. Or is it the habit of the Luftwaffe to hold back in the office as it does in the air?'

Reinhardt did not rise to the bait, merely smiled. 'You must try and forgive us, Standartenfuhrer. I am trying to adjust to a "front line" desk in Brussels. It is such a change from the nursery slopes of the Russian front. You must give me time.'

Whatever he felt at the return Kessler chose to ignore it. 'Time is something we do not have. Gentlemen, I asked you to join me here to give you the latest military information in my possession, and to draw certain conclusions, and act upon those conclusions.'

He crossed to the wall-map and drew it down a few inches before indicating the Low Countries with the flat of his hand. 'Contrary to the information disseminated by our radio broadcasts, the Allied advance has *not* halted, nor reached an impasse, nor has it been turned back upon itself. You will all have heard rumours, no doubt. It is time that we all faced up to the truth of the situation and reacted as military men and Germans of the Third Reich.' He paused. 'Yesterday Amiens fell to the enemy. Today the American forces are thirty kilometres from the Belgian border.'

The gasps of surprise were totally unfeigned.

'British armoured units are thrusting through here.' He pointed to the spearhead. 'We must assume that they will be in Brussels within one week, possibly less.'

Kessler took a packet of cigarettes from his drawer and lit one. The assembled officers took the opportunity to comment quietly among themselves.

Stroem, always the first to shine before his superior, stood up. 'Is it not possible to make a stand, sir? Better here than at the Rhine, surely?'

Keller, who Reinhardt knew only as an SD man confined to a desk, spoke up. 'The SS will work with the Waffen units, sir. Is this not our duty now?'

Reinhardt smiled to himself and couldn't restrain a chuckle

in the back of his throat. 'And what are you going to fight with? Are you expecting your small-arms issue to reply to artillery and stand up to tanks?'

But Kessler would have none of it. 'Quiet! There is no time for dissent. Whether what you say is true or not, Major, this is not the time to air defeatist attitudes.'

But Reinhardt was not to be put down. He was the only man present who had seen fighting on any front, and not merely as a Luftwaffe pilot high above the combat. He had been forced to fight his way back from the Eastern salient which had been turned into a headlong retreat. He had only just got out with his life.

'They are not defeatist, they are realist. If you can't accept ideas, then listen to some facts. There is enough ammunition in the Brussels area to supply the present garrison, and volunteers, with six rounds per man. The dump at Mollenbeek was destroyed three days ago. The Military garrison was depleted to sustain the Russian front at the same time as were the security forces. Here – in this building – we have the equivalent of three companies: not a very impressive force.'

'There will be superior forces retreating to add to the complement . . . ' Kessler rejoinded.

'Damn it, man! If they were superior forces they wouldn't be retreating!'

'That is quite enough!' Kessler stood up, his knuckles white upon the desk top, and his curious albino appearance growing pinker by the second.

'Major Reinhardt is somewhat brutal in his approach, but I believe him to be realistic. It is my assessment that we will find very few of our own fighting units retreating into the city. It would appear that they have been parted by the Allied armoured thrust. We can assume that the Allied forces will enter Brussels unopposed by any significant force. Sit down Keller! *We* are the only ones likely to do anything but retire in total confusion. We must use our initiative and muster what we can to a delaying tactic. Is there any disagreement?'

The tone of the question implied that there had better be

none. When the ebullient Keller spoke again he had accepted Kessler's leadership without argument. 'Sir . . . some of the men are already looting. What are the orders in this matter?'

Reinhardt curled his lip and muttered, 'They won't get far with their clocks and rocking-chairs. Victorious advancing armies have an unpleasant habit of moving quicker than you expect.'

Again it was Kessler who took command by sheer domination. 'In the matter of looting you have my authority to shoot the offenders. I will not have the Reich's armies looking a disgusting rabble!'

Reinhardt cocked his head and looked sideways at Kessler. Whatever one might say about the man his belief in his Fatherland was unshakeable, idealistic, and totally myopic. With more Kesslers the Nazi regime would have succeeded. With fewer Kesslers it might have been less horrendous.

Bradley returned with Natalie late in the afternoon. They had seen all they needed to at Zandvliet. At the Candide Monique pointed out the German 'tails' back at the outside table keeping a careful eye on both entrances. It proved they were right. When the restaurant opened that evening the 'tails' moved inside, sat at a table near the door, ordered beers, consumed a meal, and ordered more to drink. They intended to sit it out and not let their charges out of sight.

Security Headquarters was abuzz with activity well into the evening. Kessler's meeting continued with only a short break for coffee and sandwiches. By nine the room was thick with cigarette smoke and the officers were weary – especially the young ones. Reinhardt smiled to himself, recalling how the sixteen-year-old aircrew sent out to Russia to bolster the flagging resources had dropped into their sleeping-quarters almost before their duty terminated. The old sweats had learned to do without sleep and seemed now not to need it.

Kessler picked up the wandering thread yet again. 'Then it is clearly understood that our sole function as military men will be to perform the delaying action, to force the enemy into street-fighting that is time consuming. The British will not use their tanks or their artillery. They are intent upon preserving Brussels for posterity – whatever that may mean.'

Reinhardt spoke up calmly. 'It is not my field, Standartenfuhrer, but I would suggest that explosive charges placed at strategic points in the south and south-west of the city could imply that the entire metropolis had been similarly mined.'

'Yes, I agree.' Kessler turned his head to look at Stroem. 'Stroem, you will take charge of the assignment. Deploy the charges intelligently. I stress that – intelligently. Set the real charges where we expect the Allies to enter the city. *Pretend* to lay charges in as many places as possible in the remainder . . . especially in the central area. Be *seen* doing it. There will be eyes watching. Those eyes will report, and that report will be conveyed to the British. With any luck anticipation will hold them up more than small arms, especially if there are enough real explosions to give credence to the reports. Is that understood?

'You, Keller, will co-ordinate the transference of files and records from this building. They are to be accorded priority in vehicle transport from the city. Nothing is to be omitted. The structure of the Reich is founded upon accurate and thorough records. *No personnel* are to be given priority over the records. Is that quite clear?'

Keller understood very clearly. He knew exactly how valuable the personnel files were to the Gestapo, but only Reinhardt had a vague idea of the possibility for future blackmail – ordinary, criminal blackmail – in those tight, detailed, and devious records. He stood slowly as the others left the room and moved his chair against the wall.

Kessler eyed him ruminatively. 'Reinhardt. Have you orders from Luftwaffe command?'

Reinhardt snorted. 'I have been ordered to have all my Luftwaffe forces report to Area Command at Mortier. I dispatched all three of them the day before yesterday.'

Kessler blinked at him and frowned uncertainly. 'The remainder?'

'There *is* no remainder, Standartenfuhrer! Last month I

had eighteen men under my command. Six, I myself sent to Wing H.Q. Four have been killed by partisans. Three have gone to Mortier. Five have deserted.' He paused and then chuckled wryly. '*I* am the Luftwaffe presence in Brussels. Not, perhaps, our finest hour.'

'And our main task . . . the elimination of Lifeline?'

Reinhardt straightened. 'There, I think, I have been successful. I think, at last, I have found the key to the puzzle. It is almost academic now, but I like to bring things full circle. I think it is all centred round the Candide. Yes, Standartenfuhrer, the restaurant we have frequented for so long, and *you* have frequented for several years. In a day or so I shall prove it.'

Kessler faced him coldly. 'I don't believe it. It is too obvious a situation. I discounted it many months ago when Brandt, your predecessor, first suggested it.'

Reinhardt shrugged. There was no arguing with a man who would not be convinced. He wanted to remind Kessler of the case of Admiral Canaris, Head of the German Abwehr, relieved of his post by Schellenberg who had long been angling for it. One of the first pieces of information he received from an agent was the news of an Allied top-level conference. In his prescient wisdom Schellenberg decided 'Casa Blanca' was a feeble attempt to throw him off the scent, and informed the Chancery that there was to be a summit conference at the White House. Reinhardt smiled to himself and wished he had been present to see Schellenberg's face when it turned out to be simply a statement of fact.

Bradley peered through the clear pane yet again. The wretched tail was still sitting there.

'We can't knock him off without giving total credence to any suspicion they might have.'

'Suspicion?' Monique spat out the word. She was becoming increasingly opposed to Bradley and liked him less by the day.

'That's all it is, girl.' Bradley was so bloody positive. 'If it was anything else we'd all be kicking on the end of a rope now – or worse. Your chap got us the schedules. We have to use them *now*.

If I read it right Jerry is putting more than one rocket-launcher into Zandvliet, tonight. It has to be now! Any ideas?'

Monique thought it was nice of him to ask for once. Despite her antipathy her mind had already explored the possibilities, and she had a thought in the back of her mind. She telephoned Justine Cabot and asked if her daughter Alice could come to work in the Candide for the evening, until late, and could she come to the side door wearing a large head-scarf.

It was Maitre Guissard who put the last nail in the coffin. He needed the German Military report on the 1943 great search, when Brussels was combed by a huge contingent, searching for evaders and British agents, and during which search Albert's wife had fallen downstairs and broken her neck. The German searchers had been in the old Candide at the time. They were witnesses and totally unbiased. Guissard needed that report to collapse the case the Prosecutor was building against Albert. It was the handing of that file to be copied that brought it to Reinhardt's attention. He had not known of its existence. Now, it linked Albert Foiret, yet again, with the man Moreelse, known to be a British agent. Once brought to his attention Reinhardt shook it by the neck until he had most of what he was looking for. In his own heart he knew Albert Foiret was connected with Lifeline, possibly the man who ran it. Ordinarily, months earlier, he would have had him arrested on suspicion. But now – especially with Kessler's patronage – he had to move with caution, and in any event there could only be three or four days left to him before he, too, had to leave Brussels. Still, it would be satisfying to complete the puzzle.

When Bradley came down from his room under the eaves he had no fixed plan for getting past the tails in the square, but he knew they had to be bypassed. He glanced into the restaurant and saw Natalie working laying the table, her back towards him.

'Come on, girl. We have to leave in a few minutes, and you can't wear that dress. You'd be spotted a mile away.' he said.

'That is the whole point of wearing it, Major.'

Bradley spun round to find Natalie grinning widely at him from beside the doorway to the street. When he turned back to see the gaudy-dressed girl who was laying a table and found Alice smiling at him wearing a blonde wig that was as near as dammit to Natalie's own.

'Ve-ry good.'

Monique gave him a look as if to say, 'We aren't really all that naive.'

'It was the best I could come up with in the time.' Natalie said.

It was worth the try. Monique and Natalie/Alice left noisily amid laughter and with Monique talking volubly so that Alice's head was back to the tails view-point. Bradley watched from the window. It worked like a charm. The two tails stood up, waited, then each followed one of the girls as they separated leaving the side-door clear for Bradley and Natalie.

The Antwerp train left twenty minutes late and arrived forty minutes late, otherwise the journey was mundane. Natalie made a mental note how few German troops were now about, presumably mostly sent to stem the Allied advance.

They reached the woodland bivouac shortly before five and were met in the clearing as before.

'There isn't all that much time. Jaclyn, dig up the explosive I left with you. Tony, I want those guerilla fighters now, about a dozen.'

One thing about Bradley. He brooked little contradiction and people sensed he knew what he was about and didn't argue.

'By the way, who looks after the camp defences?' Bradley asked.

Newman looked up, slightly resentful. 'Ducane. American chap. He's a good type. Why?'

'Not good enough, I would say. I scouted-out the perimeter of this wood and your whole bloody set-up without being spotted or challenged.'

'You're wrong, man. I had a bead on you ten minutes ago.'

The dark voice came from above and was followed by two booted feet that led to the long bulk of an American flyer, rifle in hand, and wound up with a wide white grin and some dark curly hair.

'We keep a tight ship, Major. Don't you worry none. The bad guys are the Krauts. We know the difference.'

Bradley eyed him and liked what he saw. 'Okay, I take it back. Can I have *him*?'

Newman nodded as a voice from the crowd said. 'Tell you what, Major, we do a swop. You can have Ducane. Just leave us the Mademoiselle.'

Natalie smiled, but blushing as well, something that endeared her to both Bradley and Wing Commander Newman.

'Sorry. We need her. She knows the way . . . I don't.'

Guissard made a point of returning to the Havenlaan prison to see his client after leaving Reinhardt with the file he requested. Something about the German's attitude had sounded a note of alarm inside his head. Albert recognised the concern as soon as he was brought into the interview cell.

'I am sorry to worry you, M'sieur Foiret, but I have recently seen Major Reinhardt at Security Headquarters. I had gone to request the file we discussed. Undoubtedly it will finish the Prosecutor's case. There is no doubt about it. The record is full and totally exhonerates you from any contact with the deceased.' He took a deep breath. 'But something inside me says we have opened an avenue for Major Reinhardt. I ask you again: is there anything in this file likely to implicate you in . . . other activities?'

Albert frowned and discussed the course of action with the Advocate. It was a question of getting Albert out as quickly as was humanly possible. That meant a hearing before the Magistrate within the next forty-eight hours. Guissard was of the opinion he could engineer such a hearing. After he left Albert sat upon the bunk in his own cell and scrutinised his recollections of events at the time of the file incident. What was it that excited Reinhardt? What, if anything, could give the man a clue as to Albert's position and responsibility?

Natalie acted as a decoy for the German staff car that turned up unexpectedly. Bradley improvised the set-up when they heard it approaching and once the car had stopped to ascertain why a Belgian girl with a broken leg was to be found in a restricted area, they had jumped them and the motor-cycle that followed behind. The uniforms would be useful, as would the Schmeisers.

Alain had met them at the bivouac and Bradley decided that his knowledge of the land would be invaluable and put him in charge of one unit. He now led his small bunch through the undergrowth to the area behind the wooden and camouflaged stores. The trick was to get into the area without giving an alarm. There were probably thirty Jerries on the site. You needed to get rid of more than half before the balloon went up.

He glanced about him, then indicated that his group were to stay under cover while he reconnoitred, then set off on his elbows through the undergrowth, praying that the Germans did not have Dobermans, Alsatians, or any other flaming dog with them on the site. Once clear of the undergrowth he had to chance the quick run to the corner of the hut. From there he saw the lay-out clearly.

The arming section was no more than a Nissen-type hut, standing at the moment with its double-doors open and a bright, bluish light shining inside, throwing the huge object lying on its back into dramatic substance. It was one of the A-4 rockets, known to the Allies as V-2s, and it was being primed and armed before wheeling out to the Meillerwagen platform. Out there, on the concrete, one A-4 stood ready for firing thrusting menacingly up into the dark sky. The working-lights lent enough drama to the whole to make Alain suck in his breath.

Across the west side of the site, with little cover except ground scrub, Natalie crawled up to Ducane, checked watches and made a mental count-down.

The last of Bradley's little group had donned the German uniform and were climbing into the staff car.

Natalie stared at the second hand of her wristwatch. The

seconds dragged by. All she heard was the steady breathing of Ducane by her side and the distant sound of a motor vehicle. Suddenly Ducane touched her hand and pointed. She glanced up over the scrub. A German soldier was walking directly towards them. Ducane signalled and they wriggled forward to drop into a shallow ditch. The chances were the German could not see them at all in the dark, he was thrown into dim silhouette by the lights round the launching-platform. He came closer. Natalie tensed and knew that Ducane was silently drawing his knife. The sound of the vehicle drew closer. It had to be Bradley. The second hand was closing but there were three minutes to go. Then the German stopped, opened his trouser-flies, and urinated less than two feet from them. Ducane grunted silently as if to say, 'Can't you waggle it about a bit?' and she felt him hold back slightly as if to avoid any splashes. The German turned and walked away as the staff car drew to a halt by the sentry, and Bradley presented his papers. The car was permitted to enter the area and drew up outside the main hut.

Natalie released the safety-catch on her weapon and waited. Ducane spat silently onto the turf as he watched Bradley and his bunch drop from the staff car and bring up their Schmeisers. Then with a suddenness that shocked even them, Bradley kicked open the hut door and sprayed the interior with continuous bursts of fire. His follow-up went straight in the moment he stopped firing and all hell broke loose.

Natalie sensed Alain's group were attacking the actual rocket-site while she ran quickly after Ducane and another American into the workshop huts, and using their own machine-pistols on anything that moved. A metal container fell from the uppermost shelf, probably because of the vibration, and she swung round nervously to blast it full of holes.

'Easy, sweetheart.' Ducane smiled at her and then led the way hurriedly into the main area where the German troops, shocked into activity, pulled themselves together and began to fight back.

It was over in less than four minutes. Not one German was left alive to tell the tale. Thirty seconds after that Bradley and Ducane were setting lumps of plastic explosive round the sited rocket, while Alain was doing likewise with the camouflaged stockpile of five others, and the one in the machine shed.

Bradley called crisply for the detonators, and was about to be handed them when they all froze at the muffled sound of a field-telephone ringing. Without exception they all glanced about them to see where the wretched sound was coming from. It was Natalie who noticed the dull, green light flashing, no bigger than a torch-bulb, near the generator housing.

'Nick.' She indicated with her head.

Bradley bit his teeth. No answer could bring Divisional Headquarters down on them to see what was wrong. He licked his lips and made the mental decision. He knew his German was faultless, but he had no recognition-signal, no code-sign, no commonplace but necessary 'drill'. As he lifted the receiver he folded a piece of rag over the mouthpiece and took a comb from his top pocket.

As he spoke he ran his thumb-nail across the ends of the comb teeth and spoke with a built-in 'fault'. 'Station, Zandvliet . . . Hallo? Hallo? . . . cannot hear you . . . repeat, please . . . line is bad, I cannot hear . . . ' He grunted a couple of times then replaced the receiver. 'They made contact with somebody. They'll report a faulty line. There could be a dozen reasons. Let's get on with it.'

Once the charges and detonators were set for delayed explosion they got ready to move off. Alain was staring at the two German Opel 'Blitz' trucks thoughtfully.

'We could use a couple of those, you know. So could the lot in the Biesbosch. Why don't we just take 'em?'

Bradley shrugged. 'Be my guest . . . but it's risky.'

'I know where I can stash them. The Boche don't mosey about anymore. It's too dangerous for them. I'll let the lads know where they can pick 'em up.'

They reached the wood a mile-and-a-half to the south before it all went up. It was a god almighty explosion followed by four others, the last of which, presumably the stock-pile, lit up the sky. They could make out debris actually in the air. Bradley grinned at Natalie and thumped the side of the truck. Alain put his foot down, and they made towards Brussels, intending to leave the trucks under cover not too far from a railway station so they could get back reasonably quickly, certainly before the Candide closed.

What they did not know was that, after realising his mistake, the tail following Alice had gone back to the Candide, found it locked up, and then telephoned Major Reinhardt for further instructions. Reinhardt was out trying to obtain some rulings from what had once been Luftwaffe H.Q., Brussels, now no more than a holding-position for communications pending the regrouping at the fighter-station outside Evere, or the Wing H.Q. before Maastricht.

The message did not reach Reinhardt until he returned late that night. In the meantime he had been asked to investigate the rocket-site at Zandvliet where communications had broken down.

Kessler was one of the early diners at the Candide that evening. He had picked up Madeleine Duclos at her apartment shortly before eight and they took their table approximately seven minutes later. It was Alice who showed them to their table passing the Gestapo 'tail' sitting by the door glowering at all and sundry, determined to remain exactly where he was until his Luftwaffe Major turned up or ordered him to leave. Monique decided to sing earlier than her wonted time. It was that sort of evening. There was nervousness everywhere. The German predicament made everyone uneasy. No one knew what they intended. Were they going to just evacuate and leave the place to the advancing Allies? Or did they intend a more sinister termination to their period of occupation? It could be – only too easily. They all knew that Hitler had ordered Paris to be destroyed and only a miracle had saved it. What was to happen in Brussels?

The man they hated most of all, Standartenfuhrer Kessler, was in their midst, still. But no one moved or questioned or complained. They hadn't gone *yet*. It could still all go wrong for the Allies. Germany was not yet beaten, and, like most wild animals, highly dangerous in its death throes. They watched him eating, apparently unperturbed, with his mistress, and held their peace.

The trucks duly stashed away, the men dispersed. Those from the bivouacs had gone back earlier leaving Alain, Bradley, Natalie and two resistence workers to cope with the trucks. Alain left them at Hamme and went towards his farm. Bradley took Natalie's arm and persuaded her to ease up. If they were stopped now that it was well after curfew he would use his Organisation Todt Identity, rather be an adjunct to Natalie's curfew pass which would make for lengthy explanations. They did not have much time. The trains had been thrown out of gear by German commandeering for evacuation purposes. None had returned into Brussels and no one could tell them when there would be another. Natalie suggested they walk across the outskirts to the east where they might be able to pick up the suburban line that ended up in Scharbeek. From there they could walk to the Candide.

Madeleine shook her head and faced Kessler solemnly. 'No. You can't persuade me, Ludwig. I know you mean well and have my interests at heart, but I have no one else in the world. I don't want to leave you.'

Kessler placed his hand over hers, genuinely touched by the woman's obvious sincerity. No one had ever hitherto implied that they really liked him . . . never mind actually loved and needed him. His face lightened and his blue eyes smiled at her. 'You have no idea how proud and grateful I am for your saying that. I love you very much, and I want you to become my wife, but, as things stand, my dear, it would be better – well, safer – for you, if you are not the wife of a German officer.'

'Everyone knows I am your mistress, Ludwig. Would it make any difference to them when the day comes?'

'Well, that day has not come yet. It may not. The new weapons are creating havoc in England already. I have heard reports of a new bomb of unimaginable power, and there are biological weapons and nerve-gasses which are now perfected, only waiting the word of the Fuhrer to unleash. It is *not* over, it is *not*!'

Madeleine looked at him wistfully. She could see that he was trying to convince himself as much as her. She smiled and leant forward to kiss him on the cheek.

Reinhardt walked into Security Headquarters on the Avenue Louise after dropping from a tramcar outside. He, too, had found difficulty in crossing the city. The car he had commandeered for the trip to Zandvliet was required at the Military pool upon his return, and Reinhardt had let himself be taken there with the intention of walking or obtaining a tram for the last part of the journey, thus saving his driver the extra half-hour, as well as doing his tiny bit to conserve the dwindling stock of petrol. He had walked through from St Catherine's across the Boulevard Anspach, and through the many narrow shopping streets and back lanes, eventually mounting behind the Palais de Justice. In the dirty narrow streets that ran up underneath the great edifice of the Justiciary he had been stared at by German garrison patrols. They were not used to seeing one of their officers in that area alone after curfew . . . not now . . . not any more.

He had jumped a tramcar at the end of the wide avenue and stood on the outer-platform all the way.

What awaited him at his office was a pair of messages from Fürst, the Gestapo 'tail' he had borrowed. One telling him of the substitution, and the second informing him that he would await the Herr Major at the Candide that evening. Reinhardt knew that if Natalie was not at the Candide his suspicions were correct and Fürst's message proved that what he suspected was likely. He grabbed his cap once more and ran down the stairs two at a time.

A silence had fallen between them. Kessler sat back and sipped his wine, pensively watched by Madeleine. At length she spoke, quietly and tenderly: 'Ludwig. You have always been honest with me, I think . . .'

He turned to her like a startled rabbit, with a mixture of surprise, curiosity, and indignation. 'Yes?'

'Then please treat me as a grown up woman who you care for. Tell me the truth. Please Ludwig, I want to know. And it matters to me that you should *tell* me. Do you understand that?'

He stared at her face for some moments as if fighting with some internal scruple, then held her hands together for a moment before laying them down and leaving his palm on top of them. 'I do understand. You have the right to know my innermost thoughts if anyone has.' He paused again. 'When I was in Berlin I attended a small function, by invitation. There I met Speer and Borman, and we talked frankly. I have known them both for a long time. They know my loyalty and, I think, trust my judgement, as I do theirs. The war is lost to Germany, my dear. There may be delays, there may even be small victories, but the war is lost.'

She didn't look up, but after a moment a gentle smile came to her lips and she looked up at him kindly and with great sympathy. 'Thank you for being honest. Does Hit . . . does the Fuhrer accept this himself?'

'No. But if what I am told is the truth, and I have no reason to doubt it, our great leader is no longer himself. The strain has been too much – even for him.'

'You speak of him as if he were God.'

'To many of us he is no less. I have been privileged to meet him on several occasions. You cannot understand his personal magnetism, Madeleine.' Kessler's face had lit-up and it shone with a boyish fervour that was actually quite attractive, and gave substance to the inner radiance she sensed was filling him.

'I think I can. I see it in your face.'

'I would have given my life for him, willingly and with pride.'

She knew he had spoken no less than the truth, and recognised that he was deeply moved, almost ready to break down, and she could feel as never before the awe in which the real Nazi held his Fuhrer. It was something the world outside the

Reich had never understood, and never wanted to. It was that lack of understanding that was one of the main contributing factors to the terrible war which was drawing to its close. House-painter or not, Adolf Hitler had a carisma and a force that had forged his Reich into the most singleminded entity that the so-called civilised world had known since the days of Napoleon, but whereas the Little Corporal's prestige had been unable to overcome many unacceptable facets of his policy, the German Chancellor's power had been shown to be almost Divine, and capable of persuading his followers into acts of shame and degradation, cruelty and evil, not known since the days of the Golden Horde, and in many respects much more appalling than any earlier savagery could suggest.

It was at that moment that Reinhardt entered the restaurant. Kessler saw the arrival immediately and sensed that it was not a social visit, particularly when he saw Reinhardt bend over the man he recognised as a Gestapo underling and exchange words.

Reinhardt advanced towards the bar where Monique was pouring drinks for the waitress's tray. Kessler turned his head stiffly to watch. It could prove interesting – one way or the other. He didn't like Reinhardt, never had, and if he was about to make a fool of himself Kessler wanted to be an observer. But he was also a thorough and capable officer, and if he was, by some slim chance, right in his lunatic assumption, then he, Kessler, would be perfectly happy to witness that success.

Reinhardt stopped at the bar counter, clicked his heels and spoke gravely to Monique.

'Where is Mademoiselle Chentrens?'

Monique looked up at him after a moment as she finished pouring. 'Natalie?'

'Yes, Natalie Chentrens.'

'I think she is in her room, Major. She has not been feeling well today. Is it important that you see her?' She could see the glint in Reinhardt's eyes and her own heart sank.

Reinhardt's voice had an edge to it that she had not heard before. 'I'm afraid I must insist.'

'Very well, I will fetch her . . .'

Monique went into the back room and Reinhardt turned to regard the restaurant clientele who had ceased to eat, talk, drink, or do anything. They watched in tense silence. Only the slow striking of a match drew Reinhardt's eyes to where Kessler was lighting a cigarette, the back of his pink neck obstinately towards Reinhardt. The latter recognised the frightened eyes of Madeleine Duclos behind that neck and head, and bowed slightly to acknowledge her. He waited. The man Fürst stood up and ambled towards the counter and his superior, a smug expression on his face.

A slight noise made Reinhardt turn. In the doorway he could see Monique and another person. It was not Alice this time, for she was already standing by the bar, silent and tense. As she moved into the light Natalie blinked and pushed a lock of hair back across her forehead. Reinhardt's face fell, and he knew he had lost.

'May I enquire where you have been today, Mademoiselle?'

Natalie feigned puzzlement. 'I have been in bed most of the day, Major . . . Is there something wrong?'

'You left the building this afternoon with Mademoiselle Duchamps . . .'

'No. I have not been out.'

'You were followed . . . or so I understand.'

'Not I, Major. Alice said she thought a man was following her. Could it not have been her?'

Reinhardt turned to survey Alice, and sighed. 'Possibly.' He hesitated. 'I hope you are not ill.'

She smiled at him. 'Not really, just under the weather. It happens to some of us every month, Major.'

Reinhardt was conscious that he was blushing. He bowed and clicked his heels, and stalked from the restaurant followed by an anxious Fürst, very much 'tail-between-legs'.

Kessler turned to Madeleine and snorted. 'Reinhardt will make a fool of himself once too often.'

Bradley, who had entered the restaurant unobserved, passed close to Kessler, smiling, and bent over to speak.

'Good evening, Standartenfuhrer . . .'

Kessler recognised him and beamed. 'You are here late this evening, Bauleiter.'

Bradley beamed. 'Yes, it is late, for us all.'

Bradley seized Justine, the waitress, as he passed and whisked her into the small group of dancers, leaving a slightly puzzled Kessler looking after him.

4

The Allies entered the outskirts of Brussels on the 3rd of September. The spearhead forces were few in number, coming from the Guards Armoured Division and the 11th Armoured. Opposition was slight and sporadic but Kessler had been soldier enough to take the reins when the withdrawal had been general if not precipitate and he controlled the meagre resistance with surprising efficiency for a man whose military experience was almost non-existent. The charges that he had ordered planted on or around the obvious routes into the city worked. They held up the advance enough to permit the laggards to evacuate the city. Kessler himself was one of the last to leave. He ordered Reinhardt to his office for the last time.

'You will come with me, Reinhardt,'

'I have no orders to that effect, Standartenfuhrer.'

'I was given authority to command you, and others, when the situation became *in extremis*. That is what I am now doing.'

'I refuse.' The reply was bald and simple, without anger. A flat, calm statement that obviously brooked no contradiction.

Kessler glowered at him and his face reddened somewhat. 'You will do as commanded, Major!'

'I think not. The war is lost. We are overrun, man. I shall do the only sane thing and surrender to the British advance column.' Reinhardt smiled at Kessler. 'But then, *you* can't, can you? You are not a fighting man who has killed in the line of duty. Someone who can be accepted as merely a defeated enemy.

No, Kessler, it's all coming home to roost for you and your kind. Retribution they call it, I seem to remember. Would you like my gun? You once offered it to me for a similar use.'

'Major Reinhardt! You may see fit to act in a cowardly and un-German fashion if you so wish. I do not. I expressly forbid you to surrender, and once again order you to accompany me before it is too late.'

He had hardly spoken when a salvo of light artillery – possibly tank guns – was heard. It sounded very near and Kessler recognised he was without leeway. It was now or never. For him, SS-Gestapo with powers of life and death already exercised in the cause of Nazi domination, there was no choice.

'I will do one thing, Kessler. I will go to the Candide before the British arrive and I will confront Albert Foiret with what I know. He *is* Lifeline's leader, Kessler. I have proved it.'

Kessler's eyes narrowed, the original argument forgotten in the new consideration.

'Then I give you leave to go, Reinhardt. Go to the Candide and confront Foiret. And execute him.'

Reinhardt saw the keen edge of hatred in Kessler's eyes – not surprising, for Albert had been conducting Lifeline from under Kessler's very nose for almost four years.

Kessler turned on his heel without a glance at his office that had seen so much human misery, so much bellicose triumph, and so much cunning and contrivance. It meant nothing. Kessler was as sentimental as the next German – but it smelled of defeat. Reinhardt heard him stomp down the corridor and crossed to the window to watch his erstwhile colleague's departure.

Below in the street, across the tramcar lines, was the Mercedes that he had used for so long. Reinhardt could make out that the near-side front seat was occupied by a woman. It would be Madeleine Duclos who had agreed to accompany Kessler to Germany and in all probability become his wife. Reinhardt had not really understood the relationship. Mademoiselle Duclos was Belgian, from a good family. She was sensitive, intelligent – and yet she had formed this liaison with Ludwig Kessler, the most hated man in her country, and, what was more, she seemed to genuinely care for him. It was a mystery.

The Mercedes drew away and crossed the road, then turned left down the side road which would take him along the ring Boulevards and out through Woluwe and Zaventem. Reinhardt's eyes were caught by a dark mark on the road where the car had been.

When he left the Security Headquarters he bent down to look at the marks closely. As he suspected they were petrol stains. Someone had attended to Kessler's car. He chuckled and glanced across towards Ixelles, then shook his head, straightened, and set off on foot towards the centre of the city.

Albert was released from Havenlaan the same morning, just after eight. He, too, had to walk. There were no tramcars about, and from the taut sense of apprehension in the air he knew there would be none. He walked, glad of the chance to be out in the grimy, close, warm air of Brussels again, unfettered, unconfined. He was free. All charges had been dropped.

From what the friendly warder, Gavin, had told him the Allies were about to enter the city and the Germans had probably all left. There was distant gunfire – the lighter, sharper sound of transportable armour – not that of heavy artillery. Fighting was going on, somewhere – probably the roads from Tournai and Mons. They could even be already in Ruisbroek.

When he reached the Candide he let himself in. It was deserted. He walked into the restaurant and looked about him. Nothing had changed. Still the same smell that he recognised so well. It looked prosperous, cared for, inviolate, and it was still *his*. Within weeks now the British would fulfil their part of the bargain and make over to him the entire premises. It would be his in truth.

A sound made him turn and he saw the astonished faces of Monique and Natalie. They stared for a second, then Natalie ran to him saying his name over and over, and flung her arms about his neck. Monique just looked at him. They had seen each other the previous day in prison, whereas he had not seen Natalie since he was taken. He gulped at the warmth of the reception and his eyes smiled at Monique. 'Where have you been? There was no one here . . . '

'We tried to get Paul Delon to send some men. There will be trouble, you know that, don't you?' Monique said.

Albert nodded. 'That's why I wanted to be here when it happened. I didn't think I was going to make it. Just in time, eh?'

There was another sound in the back room. Albert swung round anxiously, defiantly. 'Who's that in the back room?'

'It'll be Pascal,' Natalie said.

'Pascal Keldermans? What's he doing here?'

'He's staying here for a day or so, Albert. They've already smashed all the windows in his house and surgery. Too many German patients, I think, to satisfy the locals.'

Albert was silent. 'It's only a matter of time before some tardy patriot decides to have a go at us. We'd better be ready.'

He took off his raincoat and threw it onto the bar counter, then crossed to where the Luger was kept. Before he got there the door opened and a long shadow was thrown across the check-tiled floor. They all turned and faced the Luftwaffe officer standing silent and staring.

'Major Reinhardt.' Albert almost stammered the words as Reinhardt walked slowly across the room towards the bar.

Monique and Natalie hurriedly left for the rear office, probably to hunt for a gun of some sort, yet knowing full well that their stock was in the wine cupboard behind the counter against which Reinhardt was standing.

'I had no idea that anyone was still in . . . Brussels, Herr Major. They told me that you had all retreated.'

'They have, M'sieur Foiret, all gone. All except me, I think. I am here for a specific purpose, m'sieur.'

He drew his Walther pistol and held it loosely, pointed towards Albert.

'Albert Foiret, I am now fully aware that you are the leader of the evasion-line known as Lifeline . . . '

Albert's heart sank to his boots. Dear God! minutes before the Allies arrived to liberate them and he was found out. What he used all his cunning and expertise to conceal for four years of war was now the knowledge of his enemy – and the man who had been fighting him directly for the last three months stood before him, held him at gunpoint, and confronted him with that knowledge. He knew it was useless. Reinhardt was not a man one equivocated with. He was soldier, through and through. He had fought a fairly honourable fight, and lost, only to find that – in one sense – he had finally won. Albert straightened.

'Yes, Major. I am the leader of Lifeline.'

Reinhardt's eyes never left his face for a moment. In that glance there was steel but also respect. Neither man moved a single muscle. In the back room Monique had heard the exchange and her heart, too, had sunk through her stomach and she found herself trembling uncontrollably. It was foolish, but it was happening and there was nothing she could do to stop it. Visions of Yvette, of Gaston, of Max, of faces above R.A.F. tunics, of dead helpers all flashed through her mind.

Reinhardt slowly relaxed and placed his Walther on the bar counter. 'Then I am your prisoner, M'sieur Foiret. I honour you, my friend. It would be idiocy to take vengeance now, for either of us, I think. I would prefer to join you in some of your excellent black-market brandy, and await the British here, with you . . . if I am permitted. You never know, a prisoner might come in useful.'

Albert blinked and lowered his eyes to the pistol on the counter. When he looked back at Reinhardt the Luftwaffe Major had removed his cap, was calmly seating himself on a bar-stool and waiting for a drink to be poured. Albert chuckled, more out of relief than anything, and reached automatically for the brandy bottle. It was still in the same place. Slowly he poured two very full glasses. The men both picked up the glasses and took each other's eye.

'To peace, m'sieur. And everything that matters.'

Albert nodded, they clinked glasses and downed their brandy.

When Dr Keldermans and Natalie returned from the cellars

they found Monique shaking with silent laughter. She told them what had happened, and three rather stunned people trickled into the restaurant and stared at Albert's back and the smiling Major.

'Mademoiselle Duchamps, Mademoiselle Natalie, ah . . . and the good doctor. My congratulations to you all. You played a daring game and won. I salute your courage – and I mean that.'

They realised Reinhardt meant what he said. It was not a last-minute ploy to be friendly in time for decent treatment. Reinhardt was not like that – and they knew it. It was the toast of a soldier for his peers.

When Vercors and his cronies arrived they found the Candide people drinking with a Luftwaffe officer. If Vercors needed ammunition he had it now. Natalie sensed what was about to happen and managed to slip out of the side entrance before she was missed. She ran hell-for-leather in a south-westerly direction. She knew she had to find the British, and pretty damn quick.

The altercation was quick, crude and deaf to any protest. Albert and Monique were hauled away by the growling mob amid shouts of 'Collaborator'; 'German lover'; 'Nazi whore'; and many much less wholesome abuses. Keldermans and Reinhardt were left for the second batch, under the guns of three semi-drunk patriots and a hard-faced woman 'comrade'.

It had been quick, noisy, vicious and without mercy. Keldermans was left trembling and staring at the borrowed Schmeiser MP 38. Reinhardt was saddened, amused, disgusted, and curious. His end was in sight – one way or another – and it didn't seem to matter much how. There was a nasty irony about the Lifeline people being torn to pieces by their compatriots for being 'traitors' when they had survived the German occupation and been 'excused' their transgressions by their captor/prisoner. It was all insane. The whole wretched, disgusting war was insane, criminal, obscene.

Natalie reached the British spearhead by a round-about route that avoided the half-dozen German stragglers detailed to delay by any means they could the Armoured advance. Against the real armour they had no chance, of course, but the company that spearheaded the thrust could be delayed . . . just enough.

When she made herself known she was passed along to a certain Major Turner, late of AI9, now acting under special assignment orders to make contact with the resistance and evasion-line people for the express purpose of vouching for them before their own people, who might just turn nasty where they suspected collaboration. The need for such agents was immediately apparent and Natalie was taken at her word. Without messing about Turner commandeered a car and driver, and whisked her off back into Brussels. She knew where the German snipers were and directed them by a circuitous route back towards the centre and the Grand' Place.

Turner was nobody's fool, and he wasted no time with words. The communists were disarmed without a fight. Keldermans told them what had happened, and Reinhardt was taken into custody. Again they set off in the direction of Ganz's garage: it was thought that would be where they were making for.

When they arrived the place was shut, but again Turner showed his mettle by driving the jeep right through the wooden doors. They found a near-dead Albert hanging from a chain hoist, only just breathing. The plank under his feet had been kicked away as the comrades ran from the splintering door, but it had not dropped into the well. Albert's neck was intact . . . almost.

Of Monique there was no sign. When they finally got the insensible Albert back to the Candide, and consciousness was restored after Keldermans worked on him for ten minutes, he was in such a trembling state of shock that they could get nothing from him.

Eighteen kilometres from the Diegem junction on the road to Leuven the Mercedes stopped. Kessler realised instantly what had happened, but there was no time to mess about. They abandoned the hand-luggage, and he and Madeleine set out on foot.

They had not walked for more than ten minutes when the road was straffed by Mustangs, and they flung themselves into a ditch to escape the hail of bullets and cannon-shell that spattered and burst about them. Kessler knew that without motorised transport the chance of them reaching safety was minimal. Madeleine knew this too, and urged Kessler to save himself and leave her. He refused, and they took to the wooded area on the northern side of the road to avoid being seen.

It was late afternoon when they were again upon the road, only to be forced off it when they heard straffing a short distance ahead. In fifteen minutes' time they rounded the bend and found another Mercedes staff-car sitting in the road, unmoving. Kessler approached with caution, and had almost reached the rear wing before he realised half of the vehicle was shot away – presumably by cannon fire from the Mustangs, and the occupants were either in pieces, or shot dead. He turned away, then stopped, hesitantly, and turned to examine the officer sitting next to the dismembered driver, whose remaining hand and arm were still clutching the steering-wheel. One boot caught between the accelerator pedal and the footbrake, presumably containing a foot, was all that remained of that driver. But the man next to him – a Wehrmacht Hauptman, by the insignia on his sleeve from the 43rd Artillery – was intact. Apart from a burn on the shoulder and a bullet-hole through the head the Hauptman might have been asleep and untouched by enemy activity.

From the shelter of the tree edge Madeleine watched Kessler remove his SS Standartenfuhrer's uniform and clothe himself in Wehrmacht Hauptman's, then re-dress the dead man in the discarded costume of guilt. She approached uncertainly. She didn't like death, and was frightened of it all, but the urge to survive was no less keen in her than in her lover. She watched his exchange and study the identity-papers, check the magazine of the man's Luger, reload from another, and then cast a last quick glance round to check the substitution.

They left hurriedly and made for the side of the road where they hoped to continue through the darkening hours and through the night itself. As luck would have it, Madeleine slipped on some mud and turned her ankle. Within half-an-hour it was swollen and obvious to them both that she could go hardly any further. Again she pleaded that he save his skin and leave her, but it was futile. He was determined that they would remain together. They found an empty pill-box on the roadside and rested therein.

When Albert was able to make sense, they discovered that he and Monique had been seperated outside the Candide as they were dragged away. He had not seen her again. No one knew where she could be. Albert seemed not to care, but in fairness he had been stopped on the edge of the abyss. He had looked into the face of death and been dragged back not a moment too soon. He was shattered and still trembling from head to foot whenever he thought of that moment. Natalie and Alain tried to scour the streets, but it was chaos. The British were due to arrive in greater force within the next two hours, but for the moment there was too much to do to bother with one elusive evasion-line worker. Monique was lost to them.

While they searched and worried Monique herself was being dragged into a small courtyard behind the Belvedere where a noisy mob had erected some makeshift cages of wood and chicken-wire. Terrified females were already herded into the cages while a jeering proletariat gave vent to five years of spite and fear, and spent their venom on the wretched captives. Monique glanced about her still more in shock than fear. It was just not real, not happening to her. It was something she had seen in a film, or something she had read – it wasn't happening. It *could* not be!

In the cold light of the following morning, after having spent a cold and fearful night amid the whimperings of fourteen or fifteen wretched whores whose only crime was that they had plied their trade impartially between the local customer and the conqueror, and two Belgian women who had actually cohabited with German soldiers, Monique had no doubt that it was real enough.

Shortly after nine a crowd began to gather, not closely spitting their venom into the wire-cages, but holding back, as if by command, and only spasmodic cursing crossed the gap between the victims and the avengers. Then with a growing, rumbling roar two hundred or more rabble rushed headlong down the alley leading towards the square and the cages. Their ring-leaders goaded and chanted slogans of the pathetic 'betrayal' variety, and the wretches behind the wire cringed and trembled with fear at what they expected and anticipated. They were not to be disappointed.

With a great roar of approval the first girl was dragged from her cage and brought out to a small wooden rostrum where a blotched-face man waited brandishing a pair of shears. The unfortunate creature was held down on a stool while the man clipped and chopped at her tresses until a disgusting near-bald weeping female was released to run the gauntlet.

Monique stared in horror at what was to be her fate, and she could not restrain the trembling in her limbs. Quickly she glanced down the row. If they took them in order, as they seemed to intend, she would be the tenth.

Albert stayed in bed until eleven and stared up at the ceiling. He had not slept all night. The experience had impinged upon his mind with a force that was almost impossible to shake off. Doctor Keldermans brought him some coffee and sat on the bed to talk for a few moments, then gave up the idea. Natalie was out looking for Monique, as was Alain. They had been out all night, asking, searching, pleading, but most did not know, did not want to know, and felt that, whatever they might claim, Monique was getting no more than she deserved, wherever she might be.

Natalie saw the mob running and heard the yelling about the same time as a British scout-car, bearing the Guards Armoured Divison insignia turned into the lane. The officer, Captain Stephen Durnford, nodded to his driver to explore the source of the disturbance and the car edged its way through the mob.

Natalie recognised Monique as she was dragged from the cage and force-marched to the rostrum. There was now a huge pile of hair-clippings behind the stool, and the mob had worked itself into a chanting routine, that was as hypnotic as it was frightening.

She screamed out, 'Monique!'

The voice was lost in the crowd noise, but Monique heard it and turned her head to see Natalie. Her eyes were wide with terror, but she had enough presence of mind to give a tiny negative shake of the head as a warning. She was forced down onto the stool and the blotched face barber bent over her.

Suddenly the air was shattered by a burst of machine-gun fire . . . and those near enough heard the whistle of bullets over their heads . . . not all that high. Shocked silence ensued as every head turned to see the British officer, driver, and gunner glaring at them, obviously angry and disgusted.

'Get out of here! Get back to your homes!'

There was a grumble of mild protest and some anti-British cursing. The liberators had suddenly become the oppressors. Captain Durnford snapped a command at his gunner, who primed the machine-gun again and swung it to point directly at the barber and ring-leader. The faces on that car were firm and angry, and the mob knew them for what they saw. Within seconds they started to melt away in silence. Durnford dropped from the jeep and ambled across to where a trembling Monique was clasping a weeping Natalie against her.

Durnford ordered the remainder released, then glanced at the two girls.

'You'd better get in. I'll take you near where you live.'

That was the beginning of a developing relationship between Monique and Capt Durnford. She decided never to go back to the Candide. That Albert had not found the strength to come out after the woman he was supposed to love was the last straw for Monique. She did not want to see him again – ever.

Private Wilf Ashby had learned the words – the German

words – of 'Lili Marlene' when he was in North Africa in 1942. Whenever he was sent out in 'B' company to scout with an advance column up the roads he either whistled the tune softly or broke into the German words every time he spotted a pill-box in the dark. It worked like a charm. He had winkled out more than a dozen occupants of pill-boxes all the way from Normandy to Brussels. They came out beaming with relief and walked right into the muzzle of Sergeant Cox's Sten.

This one was just like the rest. He was a Jerry Hauptman, Artillery, bit older than many, but beaming all over his albino face, just like a lamb to the slaughter.

When the Lieutenant came up and spoke to him he said his name was Spitzwerg, and he was just as surprised as the others had been. Then 'shorty' Thomas let out a whistle.

'Hey, sarge, e's got a bloody woman in here wiv 'im!'

All the squaddies turned to watch as Madeleine emerged into the torch-beams.

''Allo-'allo-'allo! 'E's been up to no good, then.'

The Lieutenant had been to college and had proper manners and knew a thing or two, and soon worked-out that the lady was unharmed, unraped, and unhappy. The Hauptman bloke shouted out that she was merely a hostage with him against her will, and the little lady bowed her head. Proper modest little thing she was.

The young officer helped her onto the tail-board of the truck and apologised for lack of better transport, hoped that she would soon get over her ordeal, and then turned to the driver to give him directions.

Madeleine looked up slowly and gazed across to where the captive Kessler stood with his guards. Their eyes met and held for the briefest of minutes. In hers was the gratitude for his final act of gallantry in disclaiming her. In his was the promise that one day . . .

The truck pulled away into the night, its blackout slits cutting the headlamp-spill to almost nothing. 'B' Company shouldered its arms and set out again with Kessler in tow, guarded only by Wilf Ashby and his carbine.

Six weeks later the Germans were fighting to keep the Allies out of the Fatherland – without much success until the winter of '44–5 brought with it such foul weather, and more than a little complacency among the American advance forces, so that when the German panzer thrust through the Ardennes started to push the American advance lines back through the snow to the area round Bastoigne there was a sudden sense of panic in the hearts of the Belgians. They would not admit to it – surely it was no more than a temporary set-back – but deep down there was the dread that the Boche would be victorious and their hated presence would again clatter through Belgian streets.

In the prison camps news leaked through that the Battle of the Bulge was going Germany's way, and once-depressed prisoners walked with heads higher and insolence again in their eyes. Kessler was no exception. He took it with equanimity when in January he was moved to another camp, not far from Brussels. This time it was a camp for officers whose identity was either not fully established or who, it was believed, might have cause to answer to a War Crimes Commission that the Allies vowed to bring into service for the once-and-for-all settlement of Crimes against Humanity.

The Camp was housed in a large ex-warehouse and supervised by Canadian troops, who regularly chaffed at the task. They were crack troops, disciplined and effective, and they resented the chore of looking after Junior German officers who were not only highly suspect, but beaten – and insolent.

Reinhardt had been sent back into a P.O.W. camp near Charleroi, but his job as Luftwaffe Police Presence in Brussels made him suspect for his possible part in criminal oppression – which was totally untrue – and overruled any kudos he might otherwise have held as a much-decorated Air Ace.

Six months after his capture he found himself being transferred to a special camp, outside Brussels, run by Canadian troops . . .

5

The Execution

The year was 1945. The month was May. It had been a rough winter with a heavier snowfall than at any time during the war. The Germans had tried to break out with the Battle of the Bulge, and, just for a moment, Europe had held its breath. Surely it couldn't happen? They couldn't win again, not after all that. But it was the death throe, the last real fight left in them, and Germany was now no more than a few square miles of rubble round a concrete bunker in Berlin.

Every morning the mist covered the ground around Brussels, hanging about, swirling, and dampening the sunlight in a way that seemed eerie – like a stage effect in 'Gotterdammerung'. That was the way it looked to Captain Prefontaine, Duty-Officer of the Molenbeek Camp for Prisoners of War Answerable for Alleged War Crimes. Krauts with records, according to Staff-Sergeant Drexler.

Captain Prefontaine looked at the timber and barbed-wire barrier across the entrance to the cantonment. Not a damned thing! Just mist and night and a tiny red glow from the butt of the bored sentry's cigarette – the one he would swear he wasn't smoking when Prefontaine challenged him in thirty seconds time. The warehouse that served as the prisoners' barracks was somewhere behind him, contained within a wired perimeter. But nobody was trying to get out. There wasn't anywhere to go, and the Canadians fed well.

As he approached the sentry-box there came the sound of an

approaching vehicle. Twin blackout slits of light glowed dimly as their feeble illumination bounced off the swirling fog. The truck stopped by the barrier.

'Hey! Lift the boom, will you? I got another bunch of Krauts.' The voice became more respectful as the driver recognised an officer approaching. 'Brigade want you to stick them with the others, sir.'

Prefontaine glanced at the sheet on the clip-board, then handed it back to the driver. 'Okay. Up with the drawbridge, Harding.'

The sentry obeyed and the truck slowly slid past the post.

'First block, second door on the right. See Staff-Sergeant Drexler,' Prefontaine ordered.

The driver nodded and urged the battered truck into the gloom inside the perimeter. Prefontaine stood still as the sentry replaced the barrier, then both of them looked out into nothing, unspeaking, unseeing, silent.

'Are you people aware we are at capacity now, Corporal? Why don't they just shoot the bastards? I've been stuck here six months because the brass and the politicos can't make up their fuckin' minds what to do with them . . . '

Prefontaine entered at the moment of profanity. 'Button your lip, Sergeant. We have a job to do. Let's just get on with it. Give the Corporal his receipt and leave the paperwork on the desk for the Commandant in the morning.'

'Sir,' the Sergeant answered smartly.

It wasn't until the Corporal left and the Duty Officer had disappeared into the inner office that Staff-Sergeant Drexler turned his attention to the new intake. Four more Germans. Jesus! There was no end to them! He sighed and picked up the clip-board.

'Which one's Rosch?'

The Wehrmacht officer clicked his heels and gave a curt bow.

'Stransky?'

A Kriegsmarine Officer stepped forward smartly.

'Walzogen?'

The second Kriegsmarine officer clicked his heels and offered a correction. '*Von* Wolzogen, bitte.'

'Yeah, yeah.' Drexler had heard it all before. 'Reinhardt?'

The Luftwaffe officer stepped forward without any acknowledgement – his eyes dead ahead.

Drexler twisted his head in the direction of the corridor and bawled, 'Lewis!'

The duty-private entered smartly and snapped to attention.

'Take these four to the pen. There's empty bunks down at the end, okay?' He turned to the Germans. 'You guys pick up your gear. Chow's at eight-hundred. March!'

The Germans followed Lewis into the corridor. They would have gone wherever he led, and with all the weary acceptance of men who have been shifted from place to place, and back again.

The warehouse that served as the prison had as its core one large room, large enough to house the entire contingent, and small enough to heat above three degrees centigrade. Bunks on two tiers stretched down both sides. The dimmed lights that remained on all night allowed the somnolent figures to appear out of the shadows here and there. Some were no more than a tiny glow of a cigarette end, others an adenoidal hole gaping and snorting above the grey blankets.

Reinhardt sat down on his bunk, and shoved his tiny kitbag at one end before heaving his boots onto the blanket and leaning back with a sigh. He didn't look about him because it just didn't matter. Curiosity had long given place to sufferance. He, too, lit a cigarette and lent his head back on his folded arm. It was his seventh P.O.W. camp. The Allies shuffled their prisoners like cards and dealt them out to whoever was handy for play.

Ever since the Liberation the Candide had done excellent business. The moment the Allied Governor lifted the German imposed curfew, and the British and Canadian officers drifted into the chairs recently vacated by the members of the Third Reich, business had prospered. Albert had done well out of the Germans – he was the first to admit it. They had been regular patrons and had behaved themselves with dignity and a slightly old world courtesy, that their cheerful and confident conquerors did not possess any more. Four years of war, the influx of allies from the New World, and a preponderance of the proletariat had smoothed over the old manners, and brought a cheerful, good-natured vulgarity to the streets of Brussels. Even the officers did not have the same hauteur as their predecessors, though English reticence made a pleasant change.

This night was no exception. The girl, Francoise, that Albert had hired to sing English songs to the new centurions – sweet, sentimental, confident Vera Lynn numbers enhanced by the French accent – was being acclaimed by the Tommies, or rather their officers, for Albert maintained his establishment for the officer class as he had done for the Germans.

Albert and Natalie were sitting half-listening to the song and taking their break when the knock came. They had been talking of Monique, of Yvette, of several who were no longer alive.

The door opened slightly and Doctor Keldermans peered round the jamb. 'May I come in?'

They were both delighted to see him and plied him with questions as they filled and refilled his glass. They talked of the latest war news, and reminisced until the old doctor turned to face Albert. 'What news of Monique?'

It was Natalie who answered. 'She is still in my apartment. She would like to see you, you know.'

'She isn't coming back?'

Natalie shook her head and avoided Albert's eyes. She knew that the affair with Durnford was not casual – never had been – and that he had asked her to marry him. After Keldermans had gone she said as much to Albert.

'She means it, then?' he asked.

'Yes. I thought you ought to know, but I don't want to talk about it.'

'I don't understand it.' Clearly Albert didn't. 'She knew I meant to marry her.'

'It was all talk, Albert. You had every chance and you kept saying "tomorrow", "next week", "next year". Then it was "after the war". What do you expect?'

'Who could tell what was going to happen? It was a stupid time for marriage.'

'That didn't stop thousands of others, Albert. Monique assumed your intention was as flexible as your timetable. And you weren't around when you were needed. Someone else was.'

'How could I leave the Candide? Everyone was going mad – they would have wrecked the place, or burnt it!'

'But it was all right if they wrecked or even burnt the woman you so desperately wanted to marry? There is something wrong with your priorities, Albert.'

Albert was silent for a moment. Then, quietly, he said, 'I didn't know where she was.'

Natalie rounded on him and glared. 'You didn't look!' She flounced out leaving Albert to nurse his bear's head and reflect on his omissions.

Every morning the German prison orderlies arrived at the Canadian officers camp from their camp north of Evere near Moelenbeek. They laid out the trestle-tables in the warehouse annexe and prepared and served the breakfast food distributed by the Canadian largesse. They were at their posts when Reinhardt walked into the annexe with Stransky, and silently joined the queue of officers lining the trestles, mess tins in hand.

They both stared at the rashers of bacon, the eggs, the waffles and the maple syrup that accompanied it.

Reinhardt glanced at his companion, 'They eat well, these Canadians.'

'Better than the French and the British, that is certain.'

Reinhardt peered at the creamy dollop. 'Is this maple syrup?'

Stransky chuckled. 'I fear so.'

'For breakfast?'

Reinhardt's comment was neither cynical nor contemptuous. No one who had existed on short rations for years was contemptuous of food – any food. It was more a surprised comment at such an availability, but instantly forgotten as they approached the urn dispensing coffee and a rich aroma that every German in the camp drank in each morning with greater avidity than he applied to his food.

They found a corner where they could sit down and eyed their companions. They were mostly junior officers. It wasn't like the other camps. This one had purpose – a purpose not yet revealed, but they all knew it had to do with war crimes. There was much talk of a huge Commission to be set up by the Allies to test, in court, the actions and reported actions of the German officer corps in their support of the Nazi regime. It was one time the responsible military were not going to walk away scot-free – and they sensed it.

Reinhardt had finished his food and was enjoying the fresh aromatic coffee when he sensed a presence standing beside him and turned to see the uniform of a Wehrmacht Hauptman. It was Kessler.

'So, Kessler. You didn't get away, after all.' Reinhardt smiled grimly. Kessler regarded him silently for some moments as Reinhardt examined the field-grey uniform.

'Hauptman Kessler, I see. Artillery. My word, how things change!'

Kessler drew himself up with the prim, steely, assumed dignity that Reinhardt knew so well. 'For perfectly good reasons I decided it was better to change my identity. My papers say that I am Hauptman Spitswerg. That is how I am known in this camp.'

Reinhardt merely sipped his coffee without comment.

Kessler continued. 'Before you – gave yourself up to the enemy – you were about to arrest the leader of Lifeline. Did you?'

'I knew it was Foiret. I went to the Candide and confronted him.' Reinhardt smiled to himself. 'He admitted it was correct.'

'You executed him?'

Reinhardt turned his eyes to look full at Kessler.

'We had a drink together. I gave him my pistol, then we had another drink and waited for the British. There didn't seem a lot of point in doing anything else. The war was lost. He was a brave man, and scared. I was a brave man, and even more scared. We didn't matter, so we drank together and waited for the end.'

Kessler's eyes narrowed and the veins in his forehead knotted momentarily. His small mouth pursed and the silver hair betrayed a slight trembling. Then he turned upon his heel and stalked away. Reinhardt watched him go then resumed his drinking of the coffee.

In a small room at the end of the annexe the German Senior Officer sat behind a tiny wooden table and stared up at Kessler. Oberst Von Schalk was an old school Junker. A man of dignity and presence. Intelligent and intimidating. Even Kessler recognised the sheer superiority of breeding as he stood before him.

'What exactly is it you are saying, Spitzwerg?'

'I am accusing one of the officers held in this detention camp of desertion amounting to treachery against the Fatherland. This officer – when ordered by me to retreat in military fashion and retrench in a more advantageous position – refused to do so. He gave himself up to the enemy, but only after making certain arrangements with a resistance organisation which he had – significantly as it would now appear – failed to apprehend.'

'Assuming that this is true, what is it you wish me to do?'

Kessler's eyes held steady and held at a point above Von Schalk's head. 'Convene a court-martial. There is not only precedent for such a court-martial, I conceive it as our duty to the Fatherland. I demand the right of every German officer to see that justice is done, and desertion and treachery properly punished.'

Von Schalk regarded Kessler with a mixture of admiration and disgust. He did not like him, but respected duty and discipline by the book. After a moment he dropped his eyes to the level of Kessler's chest and spoke in a flat monotone.

'Very well, Hauptman. You have that right. We are in extraordinary circumstances and obviously I cannot apply to higher authority for court-martial approval. As Senior German Officer I shall assume independent authority under the terms of the Army Act. I will undertake to convene a court-martial, as soon as it is convenient.'

Kessler bowed his head slightly as he clicked his heels and turned to leave the room. Von Schalk looked after him, his face quite without expression and his eyes a cold and faded blue.

Alain Muny grunted as he lifted the boxes of witloof from his trailer. They were the last and he wasn't sorry. His back was killing him and suddenly he didn't seem to have the strength he had six months ago. The weakness had been there since childhood and had made itself felt on many occasions. Then came the war and the Occupation, and it had seemed to disappear. Life was tough enough without backache. Now it was present again and he didn't like the prospect of working the small-holding with that incapacity. Gill, his brother, had done three-quarters of the work throughout the war, he would expect some help now – and it was now Alain's back was playing him up.

He crossed the pavement and entered the Candide by the main door, hurrying to dump the boxes on the counter by the bar. Albert, looked up from the bottle cupboard beneath.

'Oh, it's you.' Once again he looked down in the mouth and the circles round his eyes suggested that he wasn't sleeping as well as he might. 'Is that the chicory?'

Alain grunted and Albert straightened, then indicated a cheque tucked into the pile of glasses. Alain took it, opened and read.

'That what I owe you?'

Alain folded the cheque and slipped it into his waistcoat pocket as he nodded, satisfied.

'I'll get us a bottle . . . ' Albert turned to make for the cellar, but Alain shook his head.

'I won't, Albert, not this time. I've got calls to make. Business is moving now, there's competition. Not like it was.'

Albert turned back and Alain saw the disappointment written large across his countenance. Immediately Alain sensed the other man's loneliness, and decided to be kind.

'We-ell – half-an-hour won't make much difference. Never seem to have time to stop and drink now . . . '

'We had a lot to thank the war for. It brought people together. It's a pity it's all going so quickly.' He drew the cork and started to pour. Alain watched the dark wine filling his glass.

'You're right. Santé!' He glanced around the opulent restaurant. 'Still, you didn't do so badly out of it. It's all yours now, isn't it?'

Albert nodded philosophically. 'Yes. They were as good as their promise. They made over the deeds to me, entirely.'

'You play your cards right and you could be a big man in Brussels . . . ' He gave Albert a shrewd glance and received one in return.

'I intend to be.' The drawl was laconic, but the meaning was sharp as a knife. Albert looked him straight in the eyes. 'You know that field that joins your farm?'

'Which one, the big one?'

'The one you called "Church pasture". I want you to buy it. I saved quite a bit of money from Lifeline. You get your share. It might buy you a tractor, too. Look about. Keep your ears open. That field would treble your crop and I shall be wanting more when I open a couple of new places.'

Alain stared at him until a slow-creeping look of complicity spread across his eyes. Albert chuckled.

'Thought I was going to keep it all for myself, didn't you? No. I did very nicely with the restaurant. The surplus cash we share out between the five of us.'

'Five?'

'You, me, Monique, Natalie, Pascal. Don't suppose he wants much out of it. But we'll offer.'

Alain regarded him then slowly nodded his head repeatedly before he commenced to chuckle happily and rub his hands together. 'You know Gupy, the butcher in Hamme? He's saved a bit, too. Claimed all sorts of money from London throughout the war. This equipment, that bribe, you know. He never did a damn thing, but he got four butcher shops out of it. I dunno!'

Both men laughed and settled down to plot their moves.

At the same time exactly, some thirteen miles away, a small group of German officers were collected in the Senior Officer's quarters. Von Schalk and two majors sat at the small wooden table and faced the tall, lean figure of Major Hans Dietrich Reinhardt, Luftwaffe.

'Major Reinhardt, serious charges of a military nature have been laid against you. As Senior German Officer in this camp it has fallen to me to investigate, as well as I am able, these charges, uncover their substance, and – if necessary – convene a court-martial.'

Reinhardt stared at him unbelievingly before gasping, 'A court-martial! You can't be serious!'

'I am perfectly serious, Major. You are advised that this is to be regarded as a formal arraignment.'

Reinhardt's expression changed from cynicism to anger. 'I have known there was more than a touch of insanity abroad in Germany for quite some time. I had not realised it had spread into the Wehrmacht, sir.'

Von Schalk's face showed no reaction. 'Innuendo is a poor weapon at the best of times, Major. I am not to be drawn. You will please answer one or two questions.' He paused and coughed weakly before continuing. 'The day the Allies entered Brussels did you give yourself up to the enemy without any show of resistance?'

'What on earth can you be talking . . . '

'Yes, or no, Major?' Von Schalk's bark conveyed three generations of military authority and Reinhardt felt it right down to his boots.

'Not exactly. But in principle, yes.'

'In doing so you disobeyed a superior officer's direct order?'

'I did not acknowledge that the SS had any jurisdiction over Luftwaffe officers.'

Von Schalk cut across with the same firm voice. 'And when the opportunity arose to apprehend or destroy a known enemy of the Reich you declined to take any action whatsoever?'

Reinhardt drew himself up and waited until Von Schalk's eyes met his own.

'Am I to assume that these charges have been laid by Standartenfuhrer K . . . '

Von Schalk cut across him. 'By Hauptman Spitzwerg.'

Reinhardt snorted. 'He's no more an artillery Hauptman than I am! He's Standartenfuhrer Kessler of the SS, and Head of SS and Gestapo Activity in Belgium. I worked with him. I know.'

Von Schalk did not even blink. His eyes coldly held Reinhardt's and his voice was quiet but steely.

'Major Reinhardt, there are no Nazi personnel in this prison camp. Merely German officers loyal to their Fatherland. Is that understood?'

Reinhardt's look was withering as he surveyed the three officers facing him. He nodded several times.

'Yes. Oh, yes, that is understood . . . sir.'

'Good. Gentlemen, I am satisfied that there is a case to answer. Field Court-Martial will be convened two days from today at ten-hundred hours. Thank you. Until that time, Major Reinhardt, you will consider yourself under close arrest.'

Von Schalk stood, followed by the other two, then by his look implied that Reinhardt was dismissed. The Luftwaffe officer returned the gazes for some seconds before turning on his heel and leaving the SGO's quarters. His face was a mask of cynicism and anger, but behind it his mind shuddered with unease and vague apprehension. When he returned to his bunk he became dimly aware that two junior officers were shadowing him, keeping their distance, but always present. He was, indeed, under arrest.

Natalie's apartment was not large, but Monique had been very grateful for the chance to use it. She had not wanted to find some garret, even if she could have done so, and without income it would not have been easy. Monique did not need money at the moment. She had enough to satisfy her modest needs and, by selling Albert's presents to her, she could keep body and soul together for some time yet. Besides, Stephen kept her supplied with food and articles of clothing sent from England by his mother. He spent a great deal of time with her these days whenever he was not on duty. They slept together from time to time but Captain Durnford had a curious, old-fashioned sense of the 'right thing' and wasn't prepared to make too big a meal of things until they were properly married.

Like today, he would call round after duty hours and relax with her.

'How much tea did you put in?' He enquired after cautiously peering into the pot. Monique came in smiling from the kitchen alcove.

'Two spoonsful, and it's the tea you brought from army stores. It smells lovely . . . what's the matter with it?'

'You'll have to remember, my girl, one for the pot. I've got used to army char, and that "one-for-the-pot" matters, believe me.'

Monique giggled happily and nibbled his ear as she thumped a biscuit-tin down on the table. 'I suppose these are army biscuits, too.'

'Not on your life. My mother sent them.'

'Your mother?'

'Of course. I don't have a neat little wife to send me food parcels, do I?'

It was the wrong thing to say, of course, and he knew Monique would go quiet and moody, and she did.

'Stephen, we are going to get married, aren't we?'

'Oh, Lord! I wasn't going to tell you until later, but I'm in for a lousy afternoon if I don't, so here goes. I'm afraid its all fixed. St Xavier's. May 7th.'

Monique stared at him not quite sure if he was joking, then she sensed it was quite real, and Stephen looked a trifle sheepish. She flung her arms round his neck and hugged him as she laughed quietly, and deeply inside herself. Then the truth dawned on her.

'May 7th? But I've got nothing to wear! It's Father Maheu, and he likes things just so, and I've never been married before. Oh, Stephen, you're a brute, but I love you . . . '

They kissed, and remained in each other's arms as a knock sounded upon the front door.

'Leave it. We're out . . .'

'I can't. It might be Natalie. Well, it *is* her place!'

Stephen sighed and released her, then sank into a chair and poured himself a cup of tea while Monique crossed the room to answer the summons. She opened the door and found a woman standing before her.

'Monique?'

Monique peered at her, not quite sure who it was, for she had changed considerably, and after all one did not really expect to see the mistress of the recent head of the German Gestapo on one's doorstep, not after the liberation, not eight months after.

'Madeleine, Madeleine Duclos! Come in . . . I didn't recognise you for a moment. Please, come in.'

There was a moment's hesitation. 'May I speak to you, Monique? I shan't keep you . . .' Then she saw Stephen Durnford and faltered. 'Oh . . . I'm sorry. I'll come back another time . . .'

But Monique grabbed her arm and drew her into the small apartment. 'No, you don't. I want to know what happened to you. This is Captain Stephen Durnford, my fiancé.'

Madeleine appeared momentarily bemused as she stared at the British officer, then remembered her manners and mumbled her apologies while Monique shepherded her into the other comfortable chair and handed her a cup of tea.

'I did not mean to intrude. I was hoping to ask a favour of you . . .'

She took the cup and saucer and Monique quickly noted the frayed sleeve and the general shabbiness of her clothing, still bearing the hallmark of quality, but somehow past the end of its proper life.

'Did they . . . Did you have a bad time?'

'Not really. I did not dare go back to my flat, not for weeks. So I became a displaced person without papers – without anything really. But I've managed . . .' She hesitated and sipped her tea, conscious that she was the focal interest. Monique turned to Durnford.

'Stephen, you haven't seen much of Brussels, have you? Go and have a walk.'

'It's all right, don't mind me. I can just sit and read . . . '

Monique gave him a cold firm stare. 'Stephen! Go and change the guard or something!'

He sighed, recognised his future authority, mumbled his vague apologies to Madeleine and picked up his cap. He hovered at the door, then thought better of whatever he was going to say, and quietly closed the door behind him.

'You need help, don't you?' Monique's eyes were so full of sympathy and understanding that Madeleine was brought near to tears. Throughout the years of Occupation Monique was the only one who had shown her kindness and friendship. To the others she was Kessler's mistress – the woman who had given herself to the most hated man in the Low Countries.

'What happened?'

Madeleine knotted her fingers and commenced to relate the circumstances that had affected her from that day nine months ago when the Germans had pulled out of Brussels.

'Ludwig was as good as his word. He came for me and we left in a small civilian car. At first it wasn't too bad. We were making towards the border when two British planes flew over and started straffing the roads. There were German military vehicles retreating down the road, I suppose they were bound to do that. I was very frightened. Then the car stopped, and we found one of the bullets had punctured the petrol tank and it had all run out. All the litres of precious petrol that Ludwig had saved for just such an emergency. There was nothing to do but walk.'

'Did you have cases and things with you?'

'Only one. Just a few things I cared about. But Ludwig knew that on foot we didn't stand much of a chance. The Allied armies were not so far behind, and they had cars and tanks and things . . . Later when we were picked up, he said he was forcing me to go with him as a hostage. I wanted to cry out that he was my man, I don't care what he was or what he did . . . he had loved me and cared for me. Even at the end he was trying to save me.' She paused and swallowed some more tea. 'They took him away. I have never seen him again. They brought me back to Brussels and let me go. I think they believed him.'

'It was a fine gesture. I hated the man . . . but you know that. I'm glad he was kind to you.'

Madeleine looked up at Monique, her eyes beseeching. 'I didn't know who to turn to. I'm sorry if I have embarrassed you by coming . . .'

'I'm too vulnerable to throw stones. You don't have to make excuses to me, Madeleine. Is it money you need?'

'No . . . no. I can manage. I have one trinket left. It was given me by the Baron D'Aquise. It is quite valuable and will probably last me some time. It's not that. I . . . I need documents. Papers to get away from Belgium and start again. They won't let me leave without investigation if I can't produce any, and I couldn't. Help me, please, Monique. You used to do things like getting false papers, I know. Could you do it again, for me? And my brother?'

'Your brother? I didn't know you had a brother?'

'He could probably use his own, but, I am so frightened. If there is any way they can connect my name with Kessler, it would be impossible. I need new papers. Can you help me?'

Monique made a face and crossed to the fireplace where she rested her chin on her folded hands and considered. 'I don't see why not. The war's as good as over. Who cares any more, unless there is a reason to – like with Kessler. I'll do what I can. We managed German papers without too much trouble. I can't imagine the British are more difficult, and most of our helpers are still in their old jobs.'

'I can pay, Monique.'

Monique turned to face her. 'For a new life? That's what we all want. No money, Madeleine – for old times sake. Give me twenty-four hours. I'll have them, one way or another.'

In the Molenbeek Prison Camp the German prisoners had gathered in the warehouse area. The trestle tables had been neatly folded and set against the wall to make a large cleared area where now the entire prison complement were standing waiting. The air was tense and nervously silent. A few talked in hushed whispers until a noise from the far end caused heads to turn.

From the SGO's room Von Schalk led his senior officers to the long table placed for the court-martial. Once in place they waited for Von Schalk to seat himself. The stern Oberst glanced round the assembled men then spoke in a clear, careful, Prussian-accented voice. 'The Field Court-Martial of Major Hans Dietrich Reinhardt is now in being. It is convened through my authority as Senior German Officer in this Prisoner of War camp. I undertake the duties of President. Senior Member is Major Diffling, 33rd Artillery Regiment. Junior Member is Leutnant Schwing, 14th Panzer Regiment. Prosecuting officer is Major von Retlingen, Brussels Military District. Officer for the Defence Major Knocke, Luftwaffe. All proceedings will be duly recorded for confirmation at a later date by Oberleutnant Bahr. Bring in the prisoner.'

Several men parted to allow Reinhardt and his escort to enter and take up their positions.

Von Schalk's eyes clicked up to Reinhardt's face. 'Let us establish identity. You are Major Hans Dietrich Reinhardt, Luftwaffe?'

'I am. I wish to make it quite clear that I do not accept the validity of this court.'

'The accused's acceptance is not necessary. We will proceed. Is the Prosecution ready to begin?'

'Yes, sir.'

'The Defence.'

'Sir.'

'Then proceed, gentlemen.'

The short, lean-faced Von Retlingen stood up and the few papers in his hand shook slightly as he cleared his throat.

'The case for the Prosecution is that on the day of September 3rd 1944, the accused disobeyed an order from a superior officer, one Standartenfuhrer Ludwig Kessler, SS . . .'

Von Schalk held up his hand.

'Forgive me for interrupting you, Major. The officers detained in this camp are being held to appear before a so-called War Crimes Commission. All officers have been briefed upon our *joint* standpoint. We are purely military personnel. There are no members of any National Socialist organisation in our midst. It is the decision of this court that the SS Officer in question shall be referred to as Hauptman Spitzwerg, that being his chosen identity.' Von Schalk nodded to proceed.

Von Retlingen picked up the thread once more. 'Thank you, sir. An order from another officer, namely Hauptman Spitzwerg, and deserted to the enemy after deliberately ignoring the opportunity of apprehending a most serious and persistent enemy of the Reich.'

'Proceed to the calling of witnesses.'

'I call Hauptman Spitzwerg.'

Kessler stepped forward and took the central position facing the court.

'Hauptman, you were present in the Security Headquarters in the Avenue Louise on the morning of September the third, 1944?'

'I was.'

Describe in your own words the events of that morning relating to the conduct of the accused . . .'

While the field court-martial proceeded in all its bizarre ceremony, behind bars and without interference from the captors, Alain Muny called to see Monique at the apartment. As she let him into the room he produced several papers from inside the morning newspaper he was carrying. They were sets of exit-visas and identity-papers, all properly filled-out and stamped.

'It wasn't all that easy. We aren't geared to pinching them from the British. It's not the same . . . and we're out of practice.'

'Who got them?'

'Willi . . . who else? He's doing the same job for the British he did for the Boche. Odd, isn't it? He was more scared of losing his job if he was caught than he ever was about being shot by the Germans. People are funny!'

'Thank you, Alain. I really do appreciate it.'

'I hope you know what you're doing, love. I don't want to know who they're for, or why – just – you're getting married to a British officer. Keep your nose clean, eh?'

Monique smiled and kissed his rough cheek. Dear, dependable Alain – always there, always reliable, always discreet. When he had gone Monique put the papers in her bag. She was not wholly sanguine about what she was doing – mostly for the reason Alain had stated. She loved Stephen and wasn't going to jeopardise her forthcoming marriage if she could help it, but . . .

The door was unlocked, then there was a cautious knock and Natalie's voice. 'May I come in?'

'Hello, love, do come in. You just missed Alain.'

'Alain? What was he doing here?'

'We just talked about the wedding, you know.'

Natalie gave one of her wide gleaming smiles. 'Oh, I'm so excited! You know I don't remember anyone getting married in the whole of the war. They must have – I just don't remember any. Are you going to say anything to Albert . . . about the wedding?'

'No. I was going to go and see him. I thought I owed him an explanation – but I don't. I don't want to see him, not before the wedding. It wouldn't do any good. Besides I don't want to upset Stephen. He's too nice. I do love him, you know. We're going to be happy and live in England. He might stay in the army after the war . . . Oh, I don't know.'

'Would Albert never have asked you?'

'There was a time . . . but it was long ago. Then, when I was stuck in that cage, with my hair about to be shorn . . . and he didn't come and take me away – I felt I couldn't bear to see him again.'

'You hate him?' Natalie asked gently.

'No. Nothing. Not anything, anymore. If it didn't seem cowardly I would never see him again . . . ever. But I suppose I must. Are you all right at the Candide? You don't want to come back here? We could find somewhere else . . . '

She shook her head. 'No. You stay. I've got the old room

under the eaves. I'll come back when you and Stephen have gone to England.'

Monique grinned and kissed her cheek. 'I've got some Scotch Whisky. How about a drink?'

Leutnant Schober was on orderly detail. He had to clean up while the Court Martial was in progress. He hadn't been disciplined, it was simply his turn. The Canadians had not permitted the officers the use of other ranks as either batmen or orderlies, so they had made their own arrangements.

It was Schober's turn and he was sweeping out the tiny room and latrines down the corridor listening to the radio they had bartered for some medals and a helmet when the announcement was made that sent him rushing for the main area clutching the portable radio.

As he dashed panting into the court-martial Von Schalk turned to regard him, white with anger. 'Leutnant Schober!'

'Forgive me, sir,' stammered the agitated junior officer. 'It's the radio . . .'

'There is a court-martial in progress!'

But Schober was not to be denied. 'Herr Oberst . . . Der Fuhrer!'

The initial outrage of the man bursting into the solemnity of the proceedings suddenly stilled. Faces turned to him: eager, hopeful, frightened, apprehensive. There was hope, and there was alarm. Schober placed the radio before Von Schalk on the table and turned the volume up full.

'. . . with news coming through from Sweden. Two days earlier Adolf Hitler had made his will, and, it is understood, secretly married his mistress, Eva Braun. On the afternoon of the 30th Hitler lunched quietly in his suite, then shook hands with everyone present and retired to his private room in the bunker. At half past-three a shot was heard, and his dead body was found next to that of Eva Braun. He had shot himself through the mouth.'

The slight gasps and intakes of breath only emphasised the taut silence. The announcer continued: 'The bodies were later burnt in the courtyard, with the sound of Russian guns only a few streets away. It is understood that Hitler appointed Admiral Doenitz as his successor, but that is not yet confirmed. Meanwhile the Russians are closing in on the last pocket of resistance in Berlin. Sources both Swedish and Spanish have implied that the German final surrender is expected within the next forty-eight hours.'

Schober quietly stepped forward and switched off the following announcement. Like all the others in that warehouse he was choked with emotion. Some, like Von Schalk, maintained a solemn unyielding front, but many of the men were openly weeping. Kessler stood with head bowed in sorrow as he applied his handkerchief to the wet area below his glasses. Once returned to personal control he raised his head and glanced about him at the faces of his compatriots, before returning his gaze to the centre of the table and Von Schalk who was pale and silent and seemed unlikely to move.

'Shall we resume the court-martial, Herr Oberst?' Something of the niggling insistence in Kessler's voice was raw to many men who idolised their Leader.

One voice spoke up: 'Let it drop, Spitzwerg. I have lost the stomach for it.' Others murmured agreement before Kessler turned to face them, his eyes glowing and his expression fierce. 'If – ' and he stressed the word ominously. 'If – our beloved Fuhrer is truly dead then we have reason to mourn indeed. I have served him the greater part of my adult life, and I am proud of that honour. In the end he was betrayed, as all great men are. But are we, then, to wash our hands of it all and release *another* who betrayed him? I demand that this court be reconvened and sentence passed.'

Faces stared at him . . . and expressions hardened as they looked at Reinhardt.

'Oberst Von Schalk . . . sir, we are waiting.' No one doubted at that moment who was in charge of the proceedings. Not even Von Schalk's inbred Junker superiority held that insistent, still threatening authority of the SS Standartenfuhrer, and everyone including Count Von Schalk recognised it.

The older man breathed in deeply before speaking. 'I am reconvening this court-martial – not because that megalomaniac has died, nor because you are an incognito SS upstart. A charge has been brought against a serving officer of the Luftwaffe. We considered it our duty to test this charge in court-martial. Nothing has changed. It is still our duty. Proceed, please.'

Kessler knew the tone of voice, recognised the sentiment, but it served his purpose to let it go, and he sat down without further comment, as the Prosecutor stood up once more, and resumed his examination.

It was one hour later that the same officer concluded his case and the Defending Officer was called to make his opening statement and request witnesses. There could be only one witness so Kessler was immediately called. 'The Defence wishes to recall Standartenfuhrer Kessler.'

'I think you mean Hauptman Spitzwerg, do you not, Hauptman?'

'With respect, sir . . . this matter of service and rank is of some importance to the Defence.'

'This is a Field Court-Martial . . . You have heard the ruling. We have no time for legal niceties.' said Von Schalk.

But Hauptman Knocke stood his ground. 'Herr Oberst. A man's life may well hang upon a point which the court wishes to regard as a legal nicety. I submit that it is significant and must be admitted to the proceedings.'

Von Schalk's face registered his disapproval of the word 'must' at the same time as his mind acknowledged the point as valid. 'Request granted. The Court Recorder will ensure that no direct reference to Hauptman Spitzwerg's true identity or service is mentioned in the transcript. Is that clear?'

'Call Hauptman Spitzwerg.'

Kessler walked firmly to the central position and held his head high and still, his expression bland, as he turned to the questioning officer.

In actual distance, the point where Kessler was standing at that moment was less than fifty yards from where Staff-Sergeant Drexler sat munching a doughnut and gulping coffee as he skimmed through routine reports and appended his mark. Neither he nor anyone else had been into the 'pen' since breakfast and no one had the slightest idea of the drama being enacted that short distance away. Nor, frankly, did he care very much.

Lewis entered. 'Someone to see you, Sarge. It's a lady . . . '

Drexler did not often have his leg pulled. No one had got away with it so far, and new attempts were unlikely, so the look he gave Lewis was genuinely puzzled as well as warning.

'Honest, sarge. She's at the door, and she's a looker. Like I said . . . she's a lady.'

'You sure it's *me* she wants? Not the lieutenant?'

Lewis was insistent so Drexler hurriedly wiped his mouth on his sleeve and straightened his tie as Lewis showed Madeleine into the Duty Office. The Staff-Sergeant didn't notice the shabbiness – only that she was an attractive woman and she had 'class'. He stood up and brightened.

'What can I do for you, Ma'am?'

'I have come to ask a very big favour of you, Sergeant. I want something.'

Drexler was too old a soldier not to know when he was being propositioned, and he sniffed a profit of some sort at the same time as he let his eyes skim over her.

Her reaction was instantaneous. 'It is not myself I am using for payment, sergeant. I am not here to bargain for corned beef or a tin of maple syrup. What I want is valuable – to me, at any rate – and I am prepared to give value for value.'

Drexler's eyes narrowed slightly and he sucked his teeth as he glanced at the closed door and wondered how much Lewis could hear if the bastard was listening. 'Keep talking.' He knocked a doughnut crumb off his trouser flies. 'What sort of merchandise are we talking about?'

Madeleine straightened and took the plunge. 'I want to buy a human being. I am perfectly serious, sergeant. I wish to purchase the freedom of one of your German prisoners.'

Staff-Sergeant Drexler blew softly between his lips. 'Lady . . .

do you know what you're asking? You just sit there while I get the duty-officer . . .'

'I wouldn't do that, sergeant, if I were you. I am offering you a great deal of money for something you would not even miss.'

Mendacity had already crept across Drexler's face as he hesitated. 'How much is a very great deal?'

Madeleine opened her handbag and took out a folded parcel of tissue paper. When she opened it and revealed the contents Drexler's eyes popped out of his head. She was holding a large and very lovely necklace. The stones were small but good, and the gold setting superb, but what took Drexler's eye was the dark ruby that hung suspended in centre position. With sudden decision and the expertise of long practice Drexler's hand went straight for the desk drawer and returned holding a jeweller's eye-piece which he placed with equal dexterity into his eye socket and commenced to examine the necklace in detail.

At length he gave a long low whistle. 'It's the real thing. I give you that. What do I have to do?'

'You will arrange that a certain prisoner shall leave the warehouse undetected, and you will give me all records that he ever existed.

'Ma'am . . . I can't do that . . .'

'Sergeant. This necklace is worth at least forty-five thousand American dollars – possibly more.'

Staff-Sergeant Drexler smote his forehead and blew out his cheeks. 'Forty-five G's . . . Shit!'

Madeleine held up the necklace without moving. Drexler stared at it like a man hypnotised. When he spoke it was calm, slow, quiet, and mendacious. 'Who d'you want?'

'Hauptman Spitzwerg.'

Drexler glanced at her quizzically. 'You family?'

'You could say that.'

Drexler stood up and walked across to the window and looked out at the empty yard, the bar across the entrance, the sentry, and Mickie Dunfy, cooks' orderly, dumping the lunch waste in the bins. 'When?'

She knew she had won, and her heart beat quickly and

savagely inside her. 'Tomorrow night. Shall we say shortly after midnight?'

'Twenty-three hundred. That's when it's quiet and the officer ain't around.'

'Then eleven o'clock. Thank you, sergeant.' She picked up the necklace and deposited it back in her handbag before snapping it shut. Madeleine remained cool and businesslike.

'Where will you deliver your part of the bargain?'

'Round back of the warehouse there's a gate leads off onto the canal towpath . . .'

Madeleine nodded quickly and left the room with as little fuss as she had entered it, except that this time she waited at the door for the Staff-Sergeant to open it for her. Which he did.

The complement of prisoners stood about waiting. Some smoked the cigarettes they were allowed, a few even chatted, but most remained silent in their own thoughts. The small amount of quiet talking ceased as the SGO's door opened and Von Schalk led the court back in.

Once they seated themselves Von Schalk spoke quietly. 'Put up the accused.'

Reinhardt stepped forward with his escort, who, having placed him, retired discreetly. Reinhardt held his head well and his expression was one of curiosity rather than apprehension.

'Major Hans Dietrich Reinhardt. The finding of this Field Court Martial is that you are guilty as charged. In accordance with the provision of the Army Act governing the operations of the Wehrmacht in Occupied Belgium the sentence of this court is that you be executed by firing-squad.'

There were several gasps – not at the sentence, for the verdict carried only one penalty and they knew it, but the circumstances lent a certain piquancy to the whole thing, which was not too far removed from the ludicrous were it not so deadly serious. Kessler beamed and straightened, conscious that in his own eyes justice had been done, and, he recognised, lurking somewhere at the back of his consciousness, there existed a touch –

just a touch – of glee that he had, in the end, triumphed over a man he had never liked.

Reinhardt stood still with many eyes fixed upon him, until it slowly became obvious that the slight movement of his shoulders was occasioned by shaking with internal laughter. Slowly the chuckle came from his throat and the entire assembly turned to regard him. Von Schalk cleared his throat quietly and continued unperturbed, apparently unconscious of the illogical mirth.

'Major Reinhardt. I intend to see that the verdict of this court is properly entered in Luftwaffe and Wehrmacht records so that future times may be able to act upon the court pronouncement if they so wish. The Court is dismissed.'

'No!' Kessler's voice rang out through the warehouse. 'I insist that the sentence of the court shall be carried out!'

This time the heads turned to regard him with more than curiosity. This time there was shock as well as fear writ large on more than half the faces.

Kessler continued: 'There is no provision in the Regulations for the abandonment of a duly-passed sentence. It must be carried out, and speedily. That is our law. In view of the reported death of the Fuhrer I consider it the unparalleled duty of this court to ensure that proper retribution be made upon all traitors.'

His words caught fire in some quarters and there were two or three anonymous shouts and a smothered ripple of approval before Von Schalk raised his head. 'We have no firearms, Hauptman. Such a course is not possible to us.'

'I disagree, Herr Oberst. I feel sure that if the Canadian camp Commandant is approached in the correct military manner he will see that it is the right of prisoners-of-war to comply with a properly constituted court-martial. Will the Herr Oberst permit me to call the guard?'

Von Schalk fixed him with his baleful eyes and then turned to consider the matter with his fellow officers of the court.

In the small apartment Monique was trying on her wedding-dress, sent specially to her from Stephen's mother in England, where such things were obtainable. She and Natalie laughed and giggled like schoolgirls preparing for their first dance.

Alain had called to see Doctor Keldermans and arrange what time they would meet, who was going to do what, and also make their own arrangements for their part in the wedding. It would be that sort of wedding.

It was quite late at night when Oberst Von Schalk was given an interview with the Duty Officer. He didn't stand up and hardly lifted his eyes from the mountain of white forms in front of him.

'You wished to see me, Oberst?'

Von Schalk remained still and spoke with his quiet authority which always made Captain Hewitson feel inferior, and he didn't like it. 'It is customary for Junior officers to treat Senior officers with a certain respect – whatever the army in which they serve . . . Captain.'

Hewitson gritted his teeth, tried to subdue his blushes and slowly rose to his feet. 'Perhaps the Senior German Officer will state his request . . . sir.'

Von Schalk glanced briefly in the direction of Staff-Sergeant Drexler who was hovering in the background. Hewitson recognised the meaning, and that, too, infuriated him.

'Thank you, Sergeant.' Drexler shuffled out and Hewitson invited Von Schalk to sit before doing so himself. It was simpler that way. 'What can I do for you, sir?'

'I wish to speak with the Commandant. I understand he is in his office.'

Von Schalk pronounced the word as if it was spelt with a 'k'. He also made it sound like a polite order. Captain Hewitson hesitated but then glanced once more at Von Schalk's cold stare and decided he would sooner take a bawling out from his C.O. than stand up to Von Schalk. He stood up without further word and crossed to the inner office, knocked on the door and entered.

A moment later he returned with the tough-faced farmer

from Saskatchewan who happened to be his commanding officer and Commandant of the prison camp. Von Schalk rose correctly.

'You wished to see me, Oberst? Can it not wait until to-morrow?'

'I am afraid not, sir.'

'Okay. Then be as brief as you can, please.'

Von Schalk fixed his eyes on the Commandant's ear lobe and spoke with his customary clarity and directness. 'The officers under my command – representing the three branches of our forces – have convened a field court-martial to try, and pass sentence upon one of our number. I assure you that it has been carried out in proper fashion in accordance with the regulations of German Military law. The proceedings were duly recorded and a transcript will be available for your records. The accused has been found guilty of treasonable conduct and sentenced. Even in your army, Commandant, such a verdict carries with it the death penalty. We wish to be accorded the right to carry out that sentence.'

Clearly the Commandant didn't just accept this. He had tried to prevent shock showing on his face – without a lot of success.

'Let me get this straight, Oberst Von Schalk. You are telling me that you have held a court-martial, and you now want to carry out the death penalty?'

'Exactly.'

It was the Duty-officer who spoke, unable to contain his reaction. 'But . . . Jesus! What in hell you want to kill the poor bastard for? The goddamn war's over.'

The Commandant raised his voice. 'That is quite enough, Captain! You are addressing a senior officer.'

'You expect me to issue rifles and ammunition to prisoners in my custody?' The Commandant said it flatly, without exaggeration or innuendo – like something he didn't believe or was trying to get his tongue round.

'Four rifles – four bullets. Regulations state that sentence should be carried out as immediate as possible. We would prefer the sentence to be executed tomorrow.'

Perhaps it was the request, perhaps it was Von Schalk's manner, but whatever it was it was making the Commandant turn red and his gorge was rising inside that tight collar. Captain Hewitson waited for an explosion that did not come, and snapped to attention as his C.O. spat the words through his clenched teeth. 'Captain. At fourteen-hundred hours tomorrow you will issue the German prisoners with four rifles and four rounds. At fourteen-twenty you will collect the rifles and return them to stores.'

'But, sir . . .'

'Just do it, captain. Get Corporal Lewis to organise the making of a coffin, ready at the same time.'

Von Schalk smiled thinly and bowed slightly before he turned and walked towards the door. That was what did it. The Commandant bawled at him and stopped him in his tracks. 'I did not give you permission to go, Oberst! Now you listen to me, Von Schalk. While you are holding your little hallowe'en party I will be putting every man I have round that tin shed and every-Goddamn one will be armed with a Sten gun. If your boys come out of there shouting 'Banzai' I mow down the whole fuckin' caboodle. Is that good and clear?'

Von Schalk did not bat an eyelid.

'You may go.'

Hewitson bawled out for the N.C.O. to escort the prisoner back to his quarters before turning back to his C.O. 'Are you really going through with this, sir?'

'If they want to kill themselves why in hell not? They're crazy. The whole race – just plumb crazy! I almost wish they *would* make a break for it . . .' It wasn't under his breath, even if it was meant to be. The Commandant stomped back to his office and slammed the door as the duty-officer slumped back into his desk chair. What a night!

Outside in the darkness the ground mist swirled about and hung in heavy carpets about the forecourt and the entrance. The bar could be seen, and the sentry could be heard coughing

9

as he paced halfheartedly back and forth counting the hours till he went off duty.

In the warehouse all was silent. In the bunks the German prisoners either smoked in the gloom or slept. Reinhardt was one who did not sleep. They say men seldom do before their own execution . . . seldom want to for fear of what they might encounter in their dreams. He just lay on his bunk and looked up into the wooden slats of the bunks above him. A head appeared by his bunk edge. It was Von Wolzogen, who had accompanied him from his previous confinement.

'You're not sleeping.' He handed him a half-bottle of rye whisky. 'This might help. I don't suppose I would sleep either. No, you keep it.'

'Did our captors provide it – along with the maple syrup?'

'It cost me my medal ribbons. An excellent exchange, I think.' He hesitated, then bent over him. 'Had you thought of talking with the Canadians?'

'I imagine I am being guarded . . . discreetly, of course. Is that not the case?'

'Oh yes. I am your guard this evening until oh-two-hundred. Now is the time to go . . . if you want to.'

'Is the whisky conscience-payment, then?'

Von Wolzogen grinned and shrugged. 'No. I have no conscience. Has anyone in Germany?'

'What are you supposed to do . . . if I try?'

'Strangle you with this.' The Kriegsmarine officer held up a wire cheese-cutter, complete with wooden handles.

'Would you use it?'

'Yes. At any other time, but now I am sleepy and easy to overpower . . . ' But Reinhardt showed no interest. 'Why not?'

'If I am going to die I will go the way of a soldier – any soldier – anywhere. Not that way . . . ' He pointed to the cheese wire with evident distaste. 'That is peculiarly German.'

The sailor didn't answer for some time. 'You want to die. Don't you care at all?'

Reinhardt shrugged. 'What is there to care about?'

'Germany will rise again.'

Reinhardt gave a soft choked chuckle. 'That does not make me want to stay alive, Kapitan. Go to sleep. I will still be here in the morning.'

He turned over onto his side, presenting his back to the officer of marine who stared down at him for some minutes before withdrawing. His face expressed a mixture of suppressed excitement and blank lack of understanding.

Natalie hurried up the three steps and into the cool shadow of St Xavier's. She was almost late, and all because Albert had kept her occupied in the Candide until the last possible moment. Hastily she dipped her fingers into the stoop and genuflected as she made her way down the centre aisle. There were few people present. Stephen was already in place with his Best Man, another Captain of his regiment. Dr Keldermans was bent forward in prayer. There were three local people, merely curious, and the church helpers. Thank God, she was not too late.

She took her place alongside Dr Keldermans as the priest and his assistants reached the altar, acknowledged the Host, and turned to face the congregation.

The organ changed tune in mid-voluntary and the march announced the arrival of the bride. Stephen stood and walked to his place to await his bride. Natalie turned her head slightly to watch Monique pass upon Alain's arm. She looked very lovely and suddenly younger. Natalie bit her lower lip gently and her eyes filled with tears. It had not seemed possible that they would ever return to normality, to things like ordinary friendships and weddings. The war was almost over – things were like they were supposed to be, and the consciousness of her survival continually choked her. As she left the Candide the flower-sellers called to her and laughed as they sprayed their wares, suddenly more colourful, more ebullient, and she remembered the long queue of frightened people dressed mostly in black being herded onto army trucks at the point of Schmeissers and carbines. Jewish people, labour-camp workers. Their faces pale and resigned. Never would she sear that from her memory. Never would she cross the Grand' Place without seeing that dark crocodile of human misery. Never would she forget the whimpering silence.

The wedding was simple, the ceremony brief. Stephen, like Monique was a Catholic so there had been no problem. The organist had chosen to play the Widor Toccata for the exit and the piece thundered through the old church as they turned to walk down the aisle as Mr and Mrs Stephen Durnford. Half-way down that aisle they suddenly became aware of an extraneous sound – something that shook the building and engulfed them all. Bells were ringing. Bells, bells, bells . . . church bells . . . any bells.

Alain glanced at the others and hurried down the side aisle to the main door. He flung it open to the afternoon sun and the glorious, heart-lifting sound crashed upon his ears. Every bell in Brussels was pealing like a mad thing. Bells that had been silent for more than five years, and now they were swinging and pealing as if they had gone berserk. Flights of pigeons, startled and deafened by the unfamiliar sounds, swirled and flapped between roofs and chimneys, columns and towers.

Alain blinked at the bright sunlight, then became aware of people emerging from doorways, running down side streets, laughing and shouting and hugging each other, kissing and clapping backs.

Suddenly it dawned on Alain and he rushed back into the church, his face aglow. 'The war is over! It's . . . over.'

The single cry was picked up and echoed by every living-thing in the church. Even the priest left his place and hurried forward towards them, his pale face lit up with the Holy Spirit.

Monique and Stephen held each other and kissed quietly as Natalie and Alain embraced. Then they turned to the happy couple and kissed some more, as old Doctor Keldermans dropped to his knees and gave final thanks.

The heavy doorbolt was shot back and the doors swung open revealing to the Canadians the entire complement of German prisoners standing waiting, controlled and silent. Von Schalk was at their head as the Commandant entered.

'You still intend to go through with this?'

'Of course.' Von Schalk's flat statement brooked no possible alternative, and countenanced no real argument. It was their law, sentence had been duly passed. Now the sentence had to be carried out. The Commandant's face hardened again and he drew himself up. He and Von Schalk were both tall men.

'Okay. You have fifteen minutes. Get your men out into the yard. Once there you get four carbines and four rounds as requested.' His eyes narrowed. 'Now get this, loud and clear, Oberst. One false move, one man points the rifle the wrong way, and I open fire with Stens, Bazookas, fifty-calibres, mortars – you name it! And I'll wipe you off the face of the earth!'

There was no reaction from Von Schalk, not even the flicker of an eyelid. The Commandant turned to his duty-officer and nodded for them to proceed. The Germans filed out in orderly fashion. Reinhardt was escorted by two fellow Luftwaffe officers of his rank. He was wearing all his decorations, including the Knight's Cross. He was letting them see what he had done for his country, how he had been rewarded in the past, and how he was being rewarded now. It was all he could do, but it was very eloquent.

Outside a brick wall ran down three sides of a compound where the prisoners exercised daily. This morning it was surrounded by a hundred Canadians, all armed and grimly ready, and watching with a curious fascination. The Germans filed into a horse-shoe facing the 'open end' into which Reinhardt marched with steady measured pace, his two guards keeping a certain distance behind him. Reinhardt turned and faced his compatriots. His hands were untied and he refused the blindfold that a junior officer offered him.

Von Schalk walked silently to face him. 'Have you anything you wish to say?'

Reinhardt's grey-blue eyes fixed those of the German Colonel and held for a moment, before he cast a slow, burning glance round the assembly. 'You're mad . . . all of you. Stark raving mad!'

Kessler stood in the forefront of the assembly, his eyes bright and even excited as he watched Reinhardt. Four Leutnants armed with the Canadian rifles were already standing in position facing the condemned man.

A Hauptman took his place and holding his head high, gave the commands.

'Achtung abteilung. Laden! Sichern. Legt . . . an ent sichern.'

The four officers took aim and slipped the safety-catches as Kessler stepped forward and delivered his statement. 'Der Fuhrer befehlt . . . '

It was the ultimate insanity. A patriotic German officer highly decorated and serving on all fronts in a long and bloody war, surviving untold hardships and injury, was now being executed for sane and human behaviour, after the war was over, and in the name and wish of a leader who was no longer alive. Only Germans can behave in this way. Thus the thoughts of the Commandant who watched through narrowed eyes, his teeth clenched tight as he turned to watch the face of Reinhardt in the moment of death. He saw only a brief heart-stopping moment of fear behind the eyes before they turned up to look at the sky for a last time.

'Gebt . . . feur!'

The shots rang out and a few birds flapped and soared away from the next rooftop. Kessler stared at the crumpled body on the ground and turned, and walked away towards the entrance of the warehouse.

Suddenly there was a nearby ringing of church bells.

German heads turned to listen and Kessler stopped as he passed the Canadian perimeter guards. 'Why are the church bells ringing? I thought I heard some earlier . . . '

'The war's over, mac. Didn't you know?'

Kessler turned on his heel and walked into the confines of the warehouse, followed by the straggling and deflated Germans. Somewhere in the background the dead body of Major Hans Dietrich Reinhardt was being stowed in a cheap deal coffin and sealed. His Knight's Cross had already mysteriously disappeared.

There was a hugely festive air about the Candide that evening. Every piece of paper wrapping had been laboriously stripped and cut. From somewhere Albert had produced a box of streamers and strung a banner across the far wall acclaiming 'Victory in Europe' . . . in English for the benefit of his latest customers. Beneath it was a huge poster displaying the familiar face of Winston Churchill, complete with 'V' sign and cigar.

The place was packed. A junior British officer was pounding away on the piano. Dancers moved and shuffled, totally oblivious of the music, the tempo, or even whether or not he was playing.

One table, away from the door area – a table that had until recently been the preserve and prerogative of Standartenfuhrer Ludwig Kessler, SS, – stood empty. It was laid with care and concern and marked with a discreet notice claiming its reservation. From time to time Albert glanced in its general direction and fiddled with his tie, oblivious of the general melée of custom. When the music stopped and the applause faded as the dancers left the tiny open area that served as a dance floor he became conscious that Alain had dropped into one of the table chairs, puffing and feeling it was all much too much for him.

Natalie, laughing as ever, with her arm linked with that of a remarkably spruce Doctor Keldermans joined him and flopped into her own chair alongside. 'Oh, I could dance all night. I'm so happy.'

'I am none too sure which is worse . . . defeat or victory.' The old doctor sighed and stretched his long legs. 'I doubt if I could survive another surrender.'

'Pascal! Don't be so stuffy! You dance beautifully.' She was whisked away without protest by a pink-faced beaming Captain of Tanks.

'She's young and happy. I'm so glad. I thought the war had scarred her beyond recovery.' Keldermans said.

Albert watched them talking before his attention was distracted by a new arrival. The moment he had looked for and feared at the same time . . . it was here. In the doorway Monique and her new husband stood and surveyed the scene. For him it was the first time in a place he had heard so much about. It was the place of his new wife's past. For her it was the step back into yesterday she didn't want to make. It was the confrontation with what her life had been, and the man who had been the greater part of that life. She knew he was standing behind the bar. She had known it the moment she entered and assiduously avoided looking in that direction.

Durnford had seen Alain and Keldermans and took her arm and steered her towards their table where she could see the doctor rising to greet them. 'We were beginning to think you weren't coming.'

Monique smiled and pretended exhaustion. 'We couldn't get through the streets. Everybody's gone mad . . . they're singing and climbing lamp-posts. Oh, it's marvellous! Now, let me introduce you. Stephen this is Doctor Keldermans. Pascal, my husband, Captain Durnford.'

The old man sighed and raised his eyebrows as he regarded her. 'My dear, I realise it is a most unusual day, and on her wedding day any bride is liable to lapses of memory – but I was actually present at the ceremony . . . '

Monique giggled and made a face.

'You must treat her with concern, Stephen. I think I diagnose an acute case of happiness. Sit down, Monique. Today is more than a wedding day. It is *our* day . . . Lifeline's day. I understand there is champagne available so I have taken the liberty of ordering one bottle each to start with . . . '

Alain groaned. 'To start with! How am I going to get home?'

They all laughed until it suddenly died and Monique turned to see Albert before her. She paled, and for a brief moment her heartbeat faltered.

Albert sighed and tried to pick up the levity. 'Oh . . . don't make me feel like the spectre at the feast.'

She suddenly flashed her wide and embracing smile and her huge eyes spoke the words she was incapable of uttering. 'Hello, Albert. I don't think you know my husband. Captain Stephen Durnford – Albert Foiret.'

Both men regarded each other gravely, cautiously, and with

the polite antagonism of rivalry. There was no handshake, only the slightest of bowed acknowledgement.

It was Albert who broke the silence. 'I must congratulate you . . . both. I hope you will be very happy.' Then, as an afterthought. 'I . . . really mean that.'

Justine arrived at that moment with a huge champagne-bucket packed with ice, and with four gold-foiled bottles protruding.

'Ah. Here is our champagne.' Keldermans beamed with relief and enthusiasm. 'Albert, for goodness sake sit down.'

'No . . . ' protested Albert weakly. 'No, really, it is not possible tonight. You see all the . . . '

'I insist, Albert.' Keldermans's voice was deep and stern. He meant what he said, but Monique picked up the request as only she was able to do.

'Please, Albert. For all our sakes. You must. It is our night. Where is Natalie?'

Alain stood up and waved to her as Keldermans popped the first cork and started pouring the bubbling fluid into the glasses. Natalie arrived and whisked up a glass, as bubbly as she herself was. Before anyone could find a suitable toast or a silent moment in which to express it Durnford had risen and excused himself . . . a moment's word with a fellow officer. He put his hand on Monique's shoulder as he went, a gesture which she returned by a quick touch of her hand on his. Albert avoided as best he could watching this intimacy between them and Keldermans snatched the remaining glass.

'I think your Captain shows great sensitivity. He realises that this is something that belongs to *us*, alone.' He paused and looked sadly at the surface of his champagne. 'My friends, my very dear friends, we have survived. I not only want to thank God for His mercy . . . I want to thank you all for giving an old man's life some meaning.'

'And my life, too. We all "owe", don't we?' Natalie was suddenly still and her usual wide smile was small and gentle, saying without words the gratitude and the fear of an End that they all sensed in their hearts.

It was Alain who spoke in his quiet farmer's fumbling way. 'It's not "owing". It's more than that . . . and there aren't any words for it. It was just called Lifeline. I want to drink to all the hundreds of people who are part of that . . . '

'And to people who are not here tonight to see it . . . like this. John Curtis, Francois, Gaston, and Yvette . . . especially Yvette.' Natalie paused. 'Even Max.' She looked down at her glass and swallowed hard. The betrayal of Francois, her boyfriend, still sat heavy on her. But this was a time for other things, other thoughts. 'Yes . . . even Max.'

Albert held up his glass. 'To Lifeline, then.'

They all toasted and let the sparkling sweetness take away the pain, and the fear, and the memories. Monique's huge eyes were already flooding and Natalie tried desperately to control the trembling lip. Albert sniffed audibly. Monique turned to face him and looked directly into his eyes.

'We all have you to thank for still being alive. Don't ever think we don't realise that.'

They all murmured their agreement but Albert tried to shrug it off by proposing a new toast. 'Now. To the new Belgium, and all our new lives . . . and to Captain and Mrs Durnford.'

Albert and Monique avoided each other's eyes as they raised their glasses once more.

Stephen joined them and Monique grabbed his hand gratefully. 'They are all wishing us happiness.'

Durnford grinned. 'They are all very kind. Now . . . what have I missed?'

Doctor Keldermans handed him his glass. 'Only one glass so far. Time to top-up, everybody. There is a very long way to go yet. I have thought of at least a dozen toasts myself.'

Albert started to edge away. 'I think I should . . . ' But the attempt was doomed to failure. Alain grabbed his arm. 'You're not going anywhere, old son. Your place is with *us* tonight. To hell with the Candide, Albert. It won't run away. More champagne, Pascal.'

Natalie held out her glass and slipped her other arm through Albert's. Stephen assisted the old doctor in unwrapping the neck of the bottle and applying himself to the cork. Monique glanced up at Albert. He was looking at her.

Outside, throughout the capital, the suburbs, and the neighbouring villages, rejoicing filled the evening air. Crowds milled about, laughing for joy, singing. The tramcars hurried through the streets with an overload of happy people, all going everywhere and nowhere. It didn't matter. No one collected tickets. The bell clanged continuously. Someone had found a box of pre-war balloons and one found gaily coloured spheres and pear-shapes blowing and bounding about streets everywhere.

For the children there was no bedtime, and half a new generation was conceived that night. All over Europe the capitals and cities and towns and hamlets rejoiced as they had never done. The war was over . . . at least in Europe. The Nazi menace was no more.

No one noticed that three wretched, emaciated, forlorn figures had stepped down from the bus on the edge of Scharbeek. They clutched tiny brown-paper parcels and hoped to find their home again. To them the armistice was almost meaningless. Their millenium had arrived weeks earlier when the American and British forces advanced across Germany and found the unspeakable horror that had been their fate since being torn from their Scharbeek home in 1942. They were tired and frightened. Brussels was a long way from Belsen.

The towpath bordered the rear of the warehouse cantonment that the Canadians had turned into their Special Prison Camp. It was from the canal waters and the damp surrounding land that the mist came. It lay in billows and heavy swirling vapours for almost a mile on each side of the canal. A pair of ladies shoes, could be glimpsed, well worn and scuffed, but still shapely in the way quality goods retain their craftsmanship even when discarded. The ankles, too, were shapely as they paced back and forth in the fetid silence of the warm night. The rejoicing meant nothing to Madeleine Duclos as she paced and waited. Her concern was immediate and personal.

She glanced at her wristwatch in nervous impatience, then about her, over the top of the mist waves. Lights twinkled in the distance. The lights of Brussels, so long dead.

Behind her there came a slight creak, and she turned to retrace her steps quickly to the rusting gate in the perimeter wire. On the ground by the gate was a small well-wrapped parcel. A ham-like hand groped, found, and took the parcel. Madeleine waited.

The gate was opening and a dark figure stood there before being gently thrust through by someone else. The latter closed the gate quickly and silently and vanished into the night. The single black shape stood in the frame of the gateway and waited.

Madeleine stepped forward anxiously then broke into a run as she recognised her lover and fell into his arms. Kessler was still in his German Officer's uniform and after a long kiss and a few whispered endearments she retrieved the suitcase she had hidden in the shrubbery. Quickly Kessler changed into the unpretentious and cheap suit she had brought, tied the uniform round a large stone, secured by the knotted nylon stockings she had thoughtfully provided, and dumped it into the canal.

Hand-in-hand they walked away from the warehouse, from imprisonment, from Belgium. There would be a place for them in the new Germany. . . somewhere.

In the Candide the riotous evening was still in progress and showing no sign of abatement.

Natalie grabbed Durnford's arm. 'Stephen, will you dance with me? I don't want to ever stop dancing.'

Keldermans and Alain were already part of the tightly packed throng endeavouring to move vaguely in time with the music whenever the space was available. Alain had been collared by Justine the waitress and they had been dancing together for half-an-hour without interruption. Alain was already considering his next move and wondering how he could possibly explain it all to Estelle, his long-suffering wife. But then . . . the war didn't end every day, did it?

At the special table Albert turned from watching his customers and regarded Monique. 'You wouldn't have come to say good-bye if it hadn't been for V-E Day, would you?

'Yes, I would. I didn't want to. I'm a coward about these things . . . but I knew I had to.'

Albert lifted his eyes to look into hers. 'Why? Why?'

'Because it seemed unfriendly not to . . . I don't want . . . '

'No. I don't mean that, *Why*, Monique?'

She had been avoiding his gaze but now looked directly at him. This man had once been her life, her lover, her hopes for any future life. It was a strong, meaningful look, quickly softened by one of her female compassion. 'If you don't know, Albert, nothing I can say will tell you.'

There was a moment's silence before he spoke again. 'When did you decide?'

'I think it was the day of the landings. You took off your ring, and suddenly everything was "on". And I realised I didn't want to go through with it – not then – not now.'

'But . . . I don't understand . . . '

Monique put on her firm voice – the one that had run Lifeline in his absence. 'I don't want to talk about it, Albert. It doesn't do anything.'

He sighed and gave his very Gallic shrug. One she knew all too well. It almost made her smile as he reached into his inside pocket and produced an envelope and handed it to her.

'What's this?'

'It's your share of the Candide kitty. I've been putting it by. Alain and Natalie have theirs.'

'I don't want it.'

Albert spoke harshly. His first outburst that evening. 'You'll damn well take it, my girl! It's yours! It's the only thing that gives you independence – money. *We* want you to have it. We *insist* you take it.'

Durnford dancing with Natalie had been watching the exchange and sensed that it was time for him to intervene.

He took Natalie's hand and led her back to the table. 'It's time we left, my dear. The train leaves at six.'

Monique nodded quickly and stood up. Without another

word she stood up, kissed Natalie on the cheek and hugged her tight. Then she turned to Albert, kissed him quickly on the cheek and walked away. Durnford smiled awkwardly at everyone, then followed.

Albert watched her walk away from his life . . . through the dancers, where she stopped to kiss Alain and Doctor Keldermans. He saw her take a last quick, unsentimental look around the Candide, and she was gone.

THE END

WAR

	ISBN	Title	Price
		Heinz Konsalik	
	0427003016	DOCTOR OF STALINGRAD	60p
	0427003059	HIGHWAY TO HELL	60p
	0427003008	STRAF-BATTALION 999	75p
	0427003113	THEY FELL FROM THE SKY	75p
	0427003156	HEART OF THE 6TH ARMY	95p
	0427003148	THE LAST CARPATHIAN WOLF	75p
	0427003164	FRONT-LINE THEATRE	85p
	042700313X	THE SKIES OVER KAZAKSTAN	80p

WESTERNS

	ISBN	Title	Price
		Neil Hunter	
	0352303751	BODIE THE STALKER: TRACKDOWN	60p
	0352304014	BODIE THE STALKER: BLOODY BOUNTY	60p
		Louis L'Amour	
	042613821X	CROSSFIRE TRAIL	70p*
	0426138139	KILKENNY	70p*
	0426138562	SHOWDOWN AT YELLOW BUTTE	70p*
	0426138481	UTAH BLAINE	70p*
	0426189809	SITKA	75p*
		Frank Chandler	
♦	0426140230	A FISTFUL OF DOLLARS	60p*
		Brian Fox	
	042614015X	A DOLLAR TO DIE FOR	60p*
		Joe Millard	
♦	0426140079	FOR A FEW DOLLARS MORE	60p*
♦	042613995X	THE GOOD, THE BAD AND THE UGLY	60p*
	0426136454	THE MILLION DOLLAR BLOODHUNT	60p*
	0426131274	BLOOD FOR A DIRTY DOLLAR	60p*
	0426135490	A COFFIN FULL OF DOLLARS	60p*
	0426140311	THE DEVIL'S DOLLAR SIGN	60p*

† For sale in Britain and Ireland only.
* Not for sale in Canada.
♦ Film & T.V. tie-ins.

Wyndham Books are obtainable from many booksellers and newsagents. If you have any difficulty please send purchase price plus postage on the scale below to:

Wyndham Cash Sales:
P O Box 11,
Falmouth,
Cornwall.

or

Star Book Service:
G P O Box 29,
Douglas,
Isle of Man,
British Isles.

While every effort is made to keep prices low, it is sometimes necessary to increase prices at short notice. Wyndham Books reserve the right to show new retail prices on covers which may differ from those advertised in the text or elsewhere.

Postage and Packing Rate
UK
22p for the first book plus 10p per copy for each additional book ordered to a maximum charge of 82p.

BFPO and Eire
22p for the first book, plus 10p per copy for the next 6 books and thereafter 4p per book.

Overseas
30p for the first book and 10p per copy for each additional book.

These charges are subject to Post Office charge fluctuations.